REVEAL (FETTERED #2)

Scorpio & Harlan

LILIA MOON

COPYRIGHT

I look down at the pretty green plate heaped high with chocolate-chip cookies and topped with a cute yellow ribbon and try not to curse. It's a good thing Gabby is the nicest person I know, or I'd probably spend half my life doing stupid stuff for her. I say no to most people just fine, but she's had my number since her second day in the office.

Anyone who thinks she's just our receptionist is an idiot.

Unfortunately for me, the guys at Fettered totally know Gabby's worth, and they make sure to do good and useful things for her on a regular basis. Which means I get to play punk-rock delivery girl to her cookie-baking affliction, because apparently all good deeds in Gabby's world have to be repaid with baked goods.

I needed a walk anyhow.

I take the couple of turns down the well-disguised alley that will get me to the back door of the hottest BDSM club in town. No way anyone's on the front entrance at this time of day, and if I'm really lucky I can leave the cookies on the kitchen counter and run before anyone spots me. If Gabby wants her cookies dropped off with pretty words, she chose the wrong delivery chick.

I'm a behind-the-scenes kind of woman and everyone at Your Perfect Moment knows that. We're all in agreement that it's better that way. Stuff gets done, we keep our rep as the best wedding planners in the city, and I don't scare any of the clients with my leftover punk-rock singer attitude or fondness for black and chains. A lot of really naive, sweet, easily frightened people get married.

I get to the club's back door and discover it's already open. Or rather, it's filled with Quint's bulk as he has a conversation with Ari, who's apparently taken up tree climbing. I nod at Quint and squint up into the trees. "Is she bored, or are apple trees part of some kink I don't know about yet?"

Ari looks down at me and laughs. "This is so not an apple tree."

Details. "There are easier ways to get Quint to look up your skirt."

The big, sexy man in the door reaches for my plate of cookies and snorts.

Ari, still up in the tree, is a lot more opinionated. "You need to get laid, Scorpio. Or spanked."

I waggle my eyebrows in her direction. "You volunteering?"

She shimmies down from the tree, grinning. "Sure."

Quint rolls his eyes. "Quit recruiting—I have eleven new member requests to process this week already."

Ari laughs as she busts into the cookies. "That's totally Emily's fault. She's got all the slightly uptight ladies in town thinking they can maybe score themselves a Damon Black if they don't mind a small trip to the wild side."

I grin. My boss shook up a lot of people's world views when she hooked up with Fettered's owner. Elegant wedding planner meets spanking bench and lives happily ever after, or headed that way, anyhow.

Quint growls. "Shut up. It's my job to screen those ones and send them back to their safe little cubicles."

I pull up a very wobbly excuse for a chair and snag a cookie. "Why not just let them in? Either they'll run scared the first time they see a paddle or they'll find their inner kink and have a good time."

Ari has somehow managed to end up guardian of the cookie plate. "Emily was ready. Most people aren't. Generally we wait for people to realize what they want and seek us out."

"Exactly." Quint nibbles on his cookie like some kind of really big, blond surfer mouse. "You're nicer at telling them to go away, so you can help me work through the new member requests."

"Not a chance." Ari pats his cheek and then breaks off a big chunk of his cookie and pops it in her mouth.

"Hey." Quint swipes and misses. "Mine. You have a whole plate of cookies."

She grins at him and chews. "You big, scary Dom, you."

From everything I've heard, that's exactly what he is, but you'd never know it from his pretty-boy looks and casual demeanor. Then again, most people don't take me for the baddest wedding logistics coordinator in the business, either. Something about the spiky hair and chains seems to bias their assumptions.

Ari takes two more cookies, hands one of them to Quint, and passes the plate to me. "Damon and Harlan are in the dungeon, and Milo's hanging around somewhere."

I raise an eyebrow. "Since when did I turn into your personal delivery service?"

She snorts. "You're not mine. You're Gabby's, and I'm

pretty sure Harlan's the guy who fixed your leaky faucet, so get moving, girlfriend."

Harlan is Gabby's favorite, which means he brings his bad-boy self to my turf all the damn time to fix things that don't need fixing. He's like a house elf with tribal tats. "Last week he oiled my freaking door hinges so now I can't tell when people are sneaking up on me."

Quint laughs. "That was me—sorry."

I glare at him. A retired punk rocker can stand her ground even with the tough guys of Fettered. Somebody needs to, because everyone else in my office just rolls over and does whatever they want.

Well, except for Emily. Damon might be in charge of things in bed, but that sure as heck isn't the dynamic between them the rest of the time. He's still pretty much in awe of how she walked into his world, all sweet and bold and smart, and charmed the pants off of anyone in the BDSM community still wearing them.

It's fun to watch, even if I mostly stand on the outside looking in.

Ari tosses a thumb over her shoulder. "The cookies are getting cold. Go."

I don't want to. I want to leave them at the back door with the sassy chick who's become my good friend and the sexy Dom who doesn't make me squirm.

Because one of the guys inside? He totally does. And from the look in her eyes, Ari knows it.

Chapter Two

HARLAN

Damon's phone rings and he tosses me his wrench and gets up to leave, grinning at his screen the whole time. "Finish this up, will you, Harlan?"

I manage not to roll my eyes. Big, bad BDSM club owners aren't supposed to go all gooey when their subs call them. Which I'm smart enough not to say to my boss or any of the hundred other people I hang with who think it's totally adorable.

Emily is adorable. Damon Black all soft and gooey is... something else. He's my boss, but he's also my closest friend. For him to suddenly have a life outside the club is just plain weird.

And leaves me holding the bag on equipment repairs.

I hold up the two wrenches we haven't tried yet and sigh. Neither of them is going to fix the problem with this particular spanking bench and we both know it. Milo's the guy we need, but he's upstairs installing one of his secret projects and none of us are brave enough to interrupt him, even if it might take him days to come up for air. I lie down and stick my head back under the misbehaving bench, hoping things somehow look different this time.

"Box wrenches got you stumped?" Two feet clad in army boots stop at my shoulder. "The wrenches are the girl part. You need to find a boy part under there for them to have fun with."

I'll never look at hex bolts the same way again. "Just what I need—tool advice from a woman who spends her days tying bows around flowerpots."

One booted foot kicks my shoulder, and not very gently. "It was an emergency. Trust me, nobody lets me play with bows unless the world is close to ending."

That's not what I hear. Scorpio's pretty much the wedding planner equivalent of me—the guy who makes all the details work. I wiggle out from under the bench so I can stop looking stupid, and so that I can find out why she's skulking in my dungeon. I figure the last one out fast. She's holding a plate of cookies and they smell like pure sin, Gabby style. I grab two before Scorpio reconsiders. "She loves me best."

She sits down on the spanking bench and makes a face. "She's going through early menopause. It sometimes affects her sanity."

Gabby's a totally sexy forty-three-year-old grandmother, and there's nothing wrong with her brain or anything else. "I'm working on getting her to adopt me."

Scorpio snorts. "Get in line."

That I can believe. "Are you here to deliver cookies, or because you have a secret desire to paddle someone?"

She steals one of my cookies and makes herself totally comfortable on a piece of equipment that makes most people outside my lifestyle blush like hell. "You need a spanking, lover boy?"

Not usually. But she might—and as far as I know, she's never played. "There's no shame in wanting one."

"Duh."

I don't get her. There are always some dabblers at the club —people hanging around on the edges of BDSM and trying to decide if they really want to jump—but she doesn't smell like one of them. She's got friends who play, she's come to events here, and she's clearly comfortable bullshitting over cookies with a Dom, but she never steps all the way in.

Which suddenly has me more than idly curious. "You hang around here, but you don't play."

She shrugs, but something inside her has gone still. Watchful. "I deliver cookies. I come hang out with my friends sometimes. People here are pretty cool."

I can usually read a newbie like a cereal box, but she's twisting my wires. "Have you ever done more than talk?"

She raises a wry eyebrow. "Have another cookie and stay out of my bedroom."

That's usually an answer I'd respect, but she's got me chasing something now. People say I have the best nose in the business, and it's caught the smell of something. "You're sitting in my bedroom, so answer my question."

A long silence while she chews on a cookie and stares me down. Which is not something a Dom deals with very often, particularly one with leathers as old as mine. Finally she shakes her head. "Nah, not really. Some light kink, but no rules, no scenes."

That's the kind that sometimes goes bad in a hurry, but nobody sits on a spanking bench as calmly as she is if there are those kinds of skeletons in their closet. I decide to take her at her word. For now. "If you did, would you be a top or a bottom?" The staring has me honestly curious.

Her eyebrow does its quirking thing again. "Do you ask all the girls that question?"

Pretty much. I don't play with women who don't know the answer. I push them all into the sub role anyhow, because I know exactly what I am, and that doesn't end up a good thing for anyone who doesn't belong there. These days I'm smart enough to ask—but usually I'm pretty damn sure what they're going to say.

Not this time.

"Sub." She shrugs, but she's not quite pulling off casual. "A pretty mouthy one, though."

My imagination instantly offers up several things I could make Scorpio's mouth do if she's talking too much, and that has my brain freezing and my cock jumping to attention. I breathe, trying to get a grip. My inner Dom is suddenly *very* interested in the woman in army boots who is calmly eating her cookie and staring me down.

Damn. "I can work with mouthy."

Her eyes widen. "What?"

I've never been one of those guys who gets in the water an inch at a time. I hold up a wrench and grin. "I like girl parts."

She nearly chokes on cookie crumbs. "I bet that line gets you all the ladies."

Right now I'm hoping it gets me this one, even though my brain's clearly having trouble keeping up with some of my less complicated body parts. "You hang around, you've never played. If you want to, I'm offering. That's all."

Her eyes narrow. "Because you think I need to get in the water?"

There are some claws behind that question, and that's got my curious circuits firing again. "No. Because you're interesting. And because you're friends with the cookie lady."

She pelts me with one, straight into my forehead.

Yup, she'd eat a baby Dom for breakfast. "Pro tip—pelting your Dom with food is a really good way to get yourself tied up and punished."

She's a pretty cool cucumber, but I see the reaction. Subtle, and very quickly covered, but there. She's not wrong about being a sub, somewhere under all that self-confident sass. One who might like getting tied up a whole lot.

My cock thinks that's sexy as hell.

"Noted." She stands up, plucks something off my forehead where the cookie hit, and pops it in her mouth. "Chocolate chips taste good on you, lover boy."

I grab her wrist. Two can play at this game. Her pulse beats fast and hard under my fingers. "That's not an answer."

She's smart, and honest enough not to play dumb. "I'll think about it. I have to go—I've got six hot Italians to pick up at the airport."

I close in enough to invade her personal space. "If you ever sign my contract, you're in big trouble for that kind of sass. I'm keeping track."

She grins and twists out of my hold. "I hope you can count really high."

Chapter Three
SCORPIO

"Smile." Meghan accompanies her quiet hiss with a jab in my ribs. "You look like you want to kill Roberto. It's bad for business."

I do want to kill him. The sexy Italian with the quiet smile kissed our old front desk person and fell head-over-heels for her. Which would be fine, except now he's packing her up right after the wedding and whisking her away to his family's grape farm in Tuscany.

Okay, winery.

I'm not totally evil. I'm just going to miss Brittany.

I sidle away from Meghan and her annoying attempts to make me smile and eye the buffet table, assessing whether I'm going to starve or not.

"There are melon hearts wrapped in bacon—you'll be fine." Leo slides in beside me and grins. "And a whole lotta wine."

Roberto's family arrived well equipped, and if the last four hours are any indication, they intend to open every last bottle. Very generous grape farmers. And they adore Brittany, which means I'm going to let them do whatever they want with their wine.

Our former receptionist was one of those shy, slightly awkward people who was still growing into her own skin until Roberto walked in one day looking for the accountants next door. They say you can't change someone by loving them, but in the time it took Roberto to cross the floor to Brittany's desk, she changed herself.

And now she's going to spend the rest of her life in adorable, wine-sloshed love.

I sigh. I don't want what she's getting—a wedding full of sweet and romantic and the promise of a life barely starting. But I don't want a hot-and-dirty fling on some guy's spanking bench either.

Or I do, but I don't want what comes after that. Edges are fun, but then they end, and either you're bleeding or someone else is or you're a retired punk-rock singer standing on the periphery of a good friend's wedding and hoping a little bit of it will somehow rub off on your life.

I grip my plate a little tighter. It's a really bad idea to get all philosophical and goopy *before* the wine starts flowing. Especially when my mind won't let go of Harlan and his offer.

I don't need to play with him. I've already ridden plenty of edges in my life. Been there, got the passport stamps. I should have said no, and then I wouldn't be sitting here thinking about a sexy man and his stupid box wrenches and wondering if the high would be worth the cost that would come when we're done.

Edges have their price. It's why I'm retired and eating bacon-wrapped melon hearts at other people's weddings.

Someone in the corner starts singing, loudly and off key, and is promptly joined by everyone in attendance from the grape-farmer side of the family. Leo laughs. "I think we're gonna learn some Italian tonight."

I spent two awesome summers in Florence. "Just wave your hands a lot and keep drinking." Easiest language lessons ever.

"I don't think I can handle any more wine today." Meghan, rolling in on the other side of the buffet, looks a little green at the thought. I take pity on her—she was assigned the task of getting Roberto's parents to the wedding venue, and they probably made her drink a trunk full of wine on the way.

I grab a plate and get serious about adding some food to the wine I'm about to drink. The bacon melon hearts are stupidly cute—just the kind of thing Gabby would come up with, and probably tasty. It's hard to mess up bacon.

Behind me, someone starts clinking their fork on a glass. I turn, looking for the newlyweds, to catch the inevitable kiss.

And discover that in Italy, they're a lot more inclusive. Roberto's father reaches over and drops a kiss on Brittany's astonished mother—and then grape farmers all over the room start kissing their neighbors. I duck the questing arms of the ten year old beside me. Leo grins and plants one on the elderly woman standing beside him. Brittany's grandmother, I think.

The old woman eyes him appraisingly, and then looks at me. "He's cute—do you want him, or can I keep him?"

I'm way too used to our gay playboy videographer to bother replying.

"You can keep me, sweetheart." Leo grins at his new dinner companion. "And if you catch the bouquet, we'll run away to Bali and get married."

"Deal. I'm Tillie." She plunks a bacon melon heart on his plate, followed by a heaping scoop of potato salad, and something that looks like pulled pork. "You're not a vegetarian, are you, dear?"

Meghan shakes her head as Leo leans down and gives Tillie's cheek a kiss. One playboy, bent on making an old lady's evening unforgettable. He's a guy who lives for the shiny moments, and he absolutely knows how to create them. It's why we love him—and why he drives us all crazy.

Tillie is about to have a heck of a night.

Meghan and I, on the other hand, are either going to end up wallflowers or adopted by grape farmers who feel vaguely sorry for us. Either way I'm definitely going to end up feeling sorry for myself.

I load up my plate and wonder if I can arrange to be Tillie when I grow up, because right now the best offer I have is from a big man with tats who wants me to be his sub for a few hours. No matter how much he makes me squirm, I'm pretty sure Tillie's got the better deal.

Chapter Four

HARLAN

I walk into Damon's office a happy man. Milo has surfaced and been put in charge of all wrenches, Quint fired me from helping with member intake forms, the bar supplies screw-up miraculously fixed itself with only a couple of growls on my part, and all I have left to do today is laze around and listen to Damon and Ari have good ideas.

Life is good.

Even if I have a pair of army boots walking in places inside me they shouldn't. I sling myself into a chair and grin at Ari and the pile of paper she has in her lap. "What's that?"

She looks over at the boss. "Want me to talk about it now or later?"

Damon grins. "You can talk about a lapful of porn any time you like, babe."

That kind of talk will get you in trouble in most offices—especially if you're the boss—but not this one, at least not when Ari's on the receiving end. She was born savvy and tough and knowing exactly who she is, and she gives at least as good as she gets around here.

And if anyone ever messes with that, they'll have Damon

and me crawling up their asses so fast they'll never know what hit them. I reach over and tug on her ear, and discover that she actually does have a lapful of porn. Classy stuff, by the looks of it.

She flips over the top picture so I can't see anything good and pushes me back into my chair. "Behave. This is for a new idea I have. Some of the members have been asking for a tool to help with scenes."

I know what she's getting at, because I have my ear at least as close to the ground as she does. "Some of the old-timers are bored."

"Lacking inspiration, let's say."

And that's a problem for us, because sometimes the way they try to fix that, to bring the excitement back in, is to push boundaries. The ones that shouldn't be pushed.

Damon's clearly following the same thought track I am. "You want to use my porn collection to inspire them?"

Lots of people use it for that already—I'm pretty sure the man hardly sees most of his collection. Although I hear Emily's a fan. The man is one lucky bastard.

"Yours, mine, a few other peoples'." Ari pats her pile proprietarily. "I've picked out stuff that's juicy, suggestive, and as diverse as I can make it without getting stupid."

Anyone with ears knows Ari's view on the general stupidity of most porn and the very limited worldview of the people who usually make it. I'm smart enough to agree with her. I don't want any woman faking it with me, even if she's just on paper.

Ari starts laying out photographs on Damon's desk. "I have this all set up electronically so we can print new sets anytime. I figured Doms or subs could use it to pull a few images for scene brainstorming. Or in the case of newbies, they can get some ideas, figure out what they like. It would give them something visual to play with."

Damon's nodding, and I'm right there with him. One of the best ways to work out what arouses a sub is to let her see it, but not everyone has a dungeon full of live BDSM scenes to stroll through to gather that kind of data. Ari's photos are classy, detailed, and stimulating enough that a Dom with even marginal radar should be able to get an initial read on some of his sub's turn-ons. If he can't, he needs to go back into training. Or take up accounting. "Quint could use this for intake, too."

Damon chuckles. "That would make member contracts more fun."

"That's the whole point." Ari's got her serious voice on now, and we all know better than to fool around while she's using it. "This lifestyle isn't about floggers and restraints, it's about learning who we are and what we want, right?"

I personally like floggers and restraints quite a bit, but I manage to keep my mouth shut. Partly because she's totally right, and partly because I have a sudden idea about what I'd like to do with the pictures sprawled across Damon's desk.

I lean back, hoping like hell that I sound casual. "Can I take this set? I'll run it past a few subs, see what they think."

They both shoot me a look that says I'm not pulling off casual worth crap. Ari, however, surprises me. She calmly collects the photos, sets them in my lap, leans over and kisses my cheek, and leaves without another word.

Damon raises an eyebrow, watching her disappearing act, and then looks back at me. "I hear Scorpio came by with cookies yesterday."

Someday I'm going to get smart and work with people who don't see things. "She did. I ate them all. You want some, go find your own cookie dealer."

He just grins at me. "Emily makes fantastic cookies."

I'm pretty sure there's very little Emily's not good at. And no matter how happy it makes me for the two of them, it also scratches at something inside me. Emily's a lot more than just Damon's sub. Which wasn't something I thought was on his radar. Or mine.

I'm thinking way too hard. I like being a Dom. I pick up the photos Ari dumped in my lap. Scorpio brought me cookies. Time to go see if I can offer her some temptation in return.

Chapter Five

HARLAN

I think Gabby breaks things just for me to fix.

Or so that I'll graciously accept her cookies. Clearly she doesn't know how easy I am—or how many other motivations I have to be here. I reach for the electrical tape she's holding out to me and tap on the frayed wire in the junction box I've just freed. "You want to learn how to do this or just have me do it?"

She smiles and hops back on her stool to drink her tea. "What makes you think I don't know how to use electrical tape?"

I snort and keep doing the job she could easily do herself. "If I were smart, I'd fall madly in love with you and run off to Fiji." Sadly, I don't think a bad boy with hard edges is what she needs.

"Fiji's too far away from my girls."

It's very hard to imagine Gabby with granddaughters, but I've seen pictures. Lots of them. "Are they still demon possessed?"

She laughs. "So Jules says. They're always darlings for me."

I snort and snap off the electrical tape. "You boss around a bunch of Doms without breaking a sweat. Pretty sure you can handle a couple of two year olds."

She grins at me over her teacup. "You're always a darling for me too."

I point my pliers at her and growl. "You're the only woman in the world I let get away with calling me that."

"Again?" says a voice from the doorway. "Since when have we become tool nitwits around here?"

Gabby slides off her stool and has a pretty teacup in Scorpio's hands before she finishes her protest. "Harlan picked up the electrical tape I needed on his way over, so I figured it was only fair to let him use it."

Scorpio and I blink at each other, trying to follow that convoluted bit of logic. I toss the electrical tape at her before she can think too much harder. "Here—I'll hold the wire ends and you can wrap them."

"I can wrap something," she mutters, but she slides in under my arms to peer at the wiring for the replacement thermostat. "Sure you got that set up right?"

The thermostat is probably right. The sudden armful of woman definitely is. She smells like flowers—the dangerous ones that bloom in the night and occasionally eat unsuspecting bystanders. "Dunno. Feel free to check my work. I'll just stand here and hold things."

I can feel the moment she realizes exactly where she's standing. Even better, I can hear how her breath hitches. I bend my head down, resisting the urge to nuzzle the nape of her neck. "Take all the time you need. I like to be slow and very, very thorough."

I hear Gabby spluttering behind me, but I ignore her. If she wants Doms running tame in her office, she's going to hear stuff. Especially from me. I don't hide who I am.

An elbow digs into my ribs. No damage—just intent. A threat.

Damn feisty sub. I can feel myself grinning. I want this woman. And apparently I'm going to have to court her, which is not a game that gets played much in my world. "Put on the tape, woman."

She snorts. "Gabby, I have a recipe for cyanide cookies. I think this sexy man deserves a whole batch all to himself."

I look over my shoulder long enough to determine the woman in question has run for the hills. Or quietly snuck off because she engineered this whole thing. Never trust a grand-mother who knows how to herd small demon people. "She's gone. You're on your own."

Scorpio traces a finger over some of the ink running down my left arm, which doesn't help my patience worth shit. "She'll skewer you with a screwdriver if you mess with me."

Gabby's not my concern at the moment. "You get aroused when I get close to you."

"Don't pressure me."

I can hear the scowl in her voice. "This isn't pressure." That comes later. I don't push anyone into consent. "You seem like a woman who knows her own mind, and you haven't made up yours yet. I'm curious what's getting in your way." She's as comfortable as a newbie gets with kink. Something else is going on here.

She shimmies out of my arms and turns around, frowning. "You see a lot."

I shrug. "It's my job." I watch out for everyone at Fettered, but the subs in particular. Quint trains people, and he does a good job, but when they get out onto the real world of the club floor to play, then they're mine. Mine to watch over, mine to protect, mine to see the doubts and desires and fears they maybe don't even know about yet and make sure those things get seen and respected and met.

I want to see what's going on inside Scorpio. "You hold your cards close."

Her lips quirk. "Yup. I can beat your ass at poker any day of the week."

That isn't a good trait in a poker buddy or a sub. "Just so we're clear, that's not a safe thing in a scene." I'm watching her closely. BDSM is all about getting psychologically naked, and that scares a lot of people more than anything else we do.

It's not scaring Scorpio. Much. Her nipples are still hard, and I'm learning fast—that's her most reliable sign of interest. She's not ducking my eyes, either. "You can coach me on good scene etiquette if I decide I'm playing. Until then, I'm not your sub, so get that look out of your eyes."

Poking at her is rapidly becoming one of my most interesting hobbies. "What look is that?"

Another scowl. "The one that says you're planning on taking care of me. Lose it."

To hell with that. "That's who I am. I take care of what's mine, and you're my friend, if nothing else."

I see the mad hit her eyes—and then the pleased tenderness.

The first arouses me. The second makes me uncomfortable. There's something more complicated than some fun with a newbie swimming in the water here and I'm not sure I like it.

This is why I find my subs at Fettered. Not in nice offices with cookie-baking receptionists and women who aren't sure what they want.

But I'm here, and it's time to do what I came to do.

I reach over to the table where I dropped my jacket when I came in. "I brought something for you." I hand her the plain manila envelope. Ari's threatening to get some red silk ones, but I like the well-disguised approach. "We're testing a new tool at the club."

She takes the inch-thick package like it might be a bomb. "And I'm your tame guinea pig?"

I raise an eyebrow. "I'm pretty sure nothing about you is tame."

Her lips quirk again. "Just so we understand that."

I want to see her face when she sees what's in the package, but I'm a Dom on the hunt and she needs some time to deal with her own blockades, whatever they are. "Instructions are in the envelope."

She sets it down and studiously ignores both the envelope and my face. "Are we done taping?"

I want very badly to slide my hand under her chin and turn her face to look at me, but I don't have that right. Not yet. "For now."

She pulls the screwdriver out of my back pocket and slaps it into my hand. "Then stuff everything back in the junction box and leave it neat and tidy or we'll have to find ourselves a new guy to fix stuff that isn't actually broken."

I meet her eyes and put enough dare in them that she won't look away. "I like playing with things that aren't broken. And I never leave them neat and tidy."

SCORPIO

I plunk down on the office chair that sits in behind the old doors and plumbing pipe that serve as my desk and contemplate Harlan's envelope. I can't leave it lying around where some innocent bride might find it, because I'm pretty sure whatever's in there is intended to rile me, and I don't rile all that easily.

It's also intended to pull me across a line I'm not sure I want to cross. The one where I'd be walking the walk instead of just talking a good game.

Trading words with Harlan is fun. Whatever he's just given me, I'm pretty sure it isn't words. I pick up the envelope and undo the neat little clips holding it closed. I'm a logistics person—I don't leave things moldering on my to-do list. Which the sneaky man trying to drag me into his sandbox probably knows.

I empty the contents of Harlan's envelope on top of the piles on my desk—and then I register what my eyes are seeing and I'm very glad I didn't do this in the middle of our conference room. I push a few of the top photographs around so I can see the ones underneath.

Damn. Totally not safe for work.

Then again, I can think of more than a few brides and grooms who should look at a little porn together before they get hitched. Or after. I snicker. Maybe I can talk Emily into a totally new kind of post-wedding thank-you basket.

I pick up the small sheet of paper that fluttered out with the photos. *Pick a few images that make your nipples hard and that wouldn't be hard limits for you in real life. If you want to play with me, give me those pictures. If you don't, give this all back to Ari and tell her what you think of it as a brainstorming tool.*

Shit. Even the damn note is making my nipples hard.

I don't want to know that my nipples have been having a freaking conversation with him. And I don't want him sending me fucking porn at work.

I touch a couple of pictures, cranky and aroused all at the same time. I give Harlan credit—the stuff in here is just the way I like it. Artsy, explicit, open-minded, and real. Not all that easy to find, even if you know the right places to look.

Then I remember what he said. This is Ari's baby, and it doesn't surprise me at all that she does porn right. She might look like a sweet blonde cheerleader, but she's seriously right-eous underneath all that. A woman who knows what she wants and how to bend the big, bad Doms in her life over her knee and get it.

I grin as I see a photo that's pretty much exactly that, and wonder what Harlan will do if that's one of the ones I give him.

If I give him anything. Someone needs to learn to take no for an answer.

I sigh. That isn't fair and I know it. I haven't actually said no, and until I do, I can't expect him to read my mind.

Although he seems awfully damn good at it.

I feel my nipples tightening, just like they did when he

watched them earlier. I'm not used to being studied like that. I wish it felt like a turn-off, but it totally doesn't. Lots of people don't make it past my outer layers of punk-rocker, and they definitely don't make it far enough to ask insightful questions about why I'm hesitating.

Questions I don't want to answer.

"Whoa."

I look up. Emily's standing in the doorway and her eyes are practically bugging out. I curse the man who oiled my door hinges. I know it wasn't Harlan who did the actual greasing, but I'm blaming him anyhow. I look at Emily and decide there's no way out of this except straight through. "A little present from Harlan. I think he raided Damon's porn collection."

Amusement streaks in her eyes. "I got that part. Now tell me why he gave them to you."

I raise an eyebrow at my boss. "You've changed, lady. Three months ago you'd have turned the color of your shoes or swallowed your tongue or something."

She raises an eyebrow right back. "I hang out with the owner of a BDSM club and a bunch of people who run a betting pool on how long it will take them to make me blush."

I didn't know that. I study the amazing woman who has somehow managed to step into a totally different world and do it so well that the natives tease her like one of their own. I glance down at the photos sprawled over my work surface. "Maybe Harlan sent porn to see if he could make you blush."

She snorts, which I'm pretty sure is something she's picked up from Ari. "He'll have to get in line behind the new clients I just interviewed."

That's not usually her job. "How come Meghan didn't talk to them?"

Emily grins. "They want spankings as wedding favors."

I laugh. "Poor Meghan." Leo and I can at least talk the talk, and Gabby's holding her own in some way I don't even understand, but Meghan's the least comfortable with our new associations. Not because she has a closed mind—she totally doesn't. She's just not a fan of the ground under her feet shifting, and Fettered registers pretty high on the Richter scale.

"She's doing okay," says Emily quietly. "I'm not going to let who we are change more or faster than we can all handle."

That's why she's the boss and I'm just the chick who takes care of the details. "You're a good friend."

"I am." She sits down on the other side of my makeshift desk. "I'm also *your* friend, so spill. Why's Harlan sending you sexy pictures?"

I go with the easiest version of the truth. "They're testing a new tool for Fettered members to use. Scene brainstorming."

Emily's eyes are bugging out again. "You're going to play with Harlan?"

"Is that so hard to imagine?"

She opens her mouth to say something and then closes it again and runs her finger along the edge of one of the photos. "No, actually."

That might be more disturbing than the answer she didn't say. "He's issued the invitation. I'm pretty sure these are just meant to torment me while I ponder." And to plant very visual, very specific details in my head, damn him.

Emily's surveying the pictures now. "So you're supposed to pick what attracts you?"

"Something like that." I give her the evil eye. "It's not a group project."

She laughs, but she hasn't taken her eyes off the porn. "No, but I think I maybe need to get a set of my own."

Oh yeah—Emily's changed. Big time.

Which is part of my problem. I'm not sure I want to. Not

all fast rides are heading in a good direction, and I don't know where I want this one to go, or whether I even get to pick. Harlan doesn't seem like a guy used to sharing the steering wheel. I sweep up the photos and stuff them back in the envelope, and then I swing past my startled, grinning boss and head for the door. "I'm going to see a man about a thing."

If he can bring this to my turf, I can damn well take it to his. And I don't need electrical tape as an excuse.

The walking distance between our offices and Fettered is just about right to work up a good head of steam. I know because this isn't the first time I've arrived at the club pissy and on edge.

I am, however, pissy and honest. Harlan sending me porn at work is not the problem here. That doesn't mean I'm going to give him a free pass. I head in the front door this time and wave at Ari and Quint at the bar as I pass through the outer sanctum. "Looking for Harlan. I'll catch you in a bit."

Ari looks up from a stack of paperwork taller than her drink. "I don't think he's in the dungeon."

Quint shakes his head. "He's in one of the private rooms with Milo, installing the new sex chair."

Ari grins. "That chair rocks. I need to find someone to lock me up and ravish me."

Quint ruffles her hair. "Sorry, darlin'. I'm busy tonight."

I grin at both of them. "You guys have really weird work conversations, you know that?"

"What?" Ari shrugs her shoulders and gives me an intentionally clueless look. "You can watch if you want."

She knows I don't want. "I'm one of those annoying types who comes here to drink your cocktails and mingle with the interesting people and doesn't actually step up and do anything fun."

Quint pours what looks like lemonade into a glass and pushes it across the bar in my direction. "You're not a tourist —you're a friend. There's a difference."

Damn the Doms of this place and their ability to see right through me. "Thanks."

He nods his head at a stool. "Sit. Drink. I'll let Harlan know you're here."

I give up and slide onto the stool. Quint makes killer lemonade, and I'm a smart enough tourist to know better than to walk into one of Fettered's private rooms, no matter what the people inside claimed they were going to be doing.

Ari watches Quint walk away, and then gives me the kind of look that says I'm not out of the frying pan yet. "What's up with you and Harlan?"

That's not something I know how to answer. "He wants to know why I don't play."

She sips her lemonade. "Fair question. Do you know the answer?"

"Yeah." I can lemonade-sip anyone under the table.

She waits a moment and then laughs. "Gee, Scorpio, do you want to talk about it?"

Probably not. "Tell me about Milo's new chair."

She flutters her eyelashes at me. "I can give you a tour later."

Easily one of the coolest things about Ari is her flexible, wide-open generosity. She'll consider doing almost anything that might help someone else be a more fulfilled human being, and even though she's making this offer as a joke, I also know she'd be willing to make it real in a heartbeat.

I squeeze her hand. "Thanks."

She sobers, and her eyes are smart and wise and compassionate. "It's gotten real, huh?"

It has. I hear footsteps behind us, and know without looking that real has just arrived. Ari slides off her stool and picks up her paperwork and lemonade. "I have stuff to go take care of."

Harlan's voice rumbles at my back. "Milo could use help testing the restraint mechanisms."

Ari snorts. "This time I'm locking him up first."

I laugh. I've heard that story. Being Milo's alpha tester is a risky job.

She slips away, and the footsteps behind me get closer. "I didn't expect to see you here."

I slap his envelope down on the bar. "Really? You bring me porn at work and figure I'm just going to obediently drop a few pictures in your mailbox?"

He shrugs, pours himself some lemonade, and slides onto a stool beside me. "Maybe."

Being this close to him is like holding an electric guitar right before the first chords rip. He's always made me sit up and take notice, but it's getting more potent. I've never had a problem appreciating a big, sexy bad boy—muscles and ink are both in my happy zone. But this is more than that.

He sees me, pushes on me, and those are a totally different kind of electricity.

He puts his hand on the envelope. "Did you look?"

"Yeah."

He drinks his lemonade and doesn't say anything.

He also knows when not to push, and that makes it a lot harder to stay pissy. "I was at a wedding a couple of days ago. Brittany, our old receptionist. She hooked up with a grape farmer and now she's heading off to Tuscany to eat spaghetti and have many babies and be stupidly happy."

He's grinning. "Some parts of that sound pretty good."

I close my eyes. One smart-ass comment and he's nailed it. "That's just it. There are parts of that I want." I sweep my hand around the club lounge. "And parts of this I want. And parts of the punk-rocker musician thing I did for ten years that I want. But none of them are mostly right, if that makes any sense."

I open my eyes to find him studying me, intense and serious. He lifts a hand and barely touches the nape of my neck. "Why'd you stop the music?"

The man who sends me porn and makes my neck yearn probably deserves something more than my usual pat answer. "I loved making music. I played lead guitar, was a solid back-up singer, wrote some of the songs. My band was pretty good— good enough to keep ourselves fed if we worked hard at it." Most musicians couldn't say the same thing, so by our own standards, we were a success. "It was the in-between that was hard. We rode the good edges with the music, and too many of the bad edges when we weren't playing."

Still with the intent eyes. "Drugs?"

"That and a bunch of other stuff. Not my thing, mostly, but I watched a lot of friends self-destruct. There was nowhere good and fulfilling to go between the music. Nowhere to live that wasn't an edge. Too much emptiness and too much bleeding." I can feel the exhausted loneliness rising in my ribs just talking about it.

His hand slides down my back. "So you found a way out."

"One day Emily overheard me sorting out gig logistics with some guy at a bar and offered me a job. I thought she was a raving lunatic."

Harlan's cheek dimples. "But you took it."

I shrug. "The pay was good, and she promised I could wear whatever I wanted to work and use as many curse words as I needed to get the job done." And something in her eyes had promised to be my friend.

She still doesn't know that's the part that sealed the deal.

His hand is stroking my back like I'm an oversized kitten. "That's why Damon opened Fettered."

I blink, and finally meet his intense eyes head-on. "What?"

"Lots of people in the BDSM world are living edge to edge. Fettered supports doing that safely, but it's also the good and safe place to come in between. That's why we have squishy couches and *Pictionary* nights and people dropping in all the damn time just to talk."

I'd seen all that and assumed it was just part of Damon's very smart marketing plan. "It's a family."

He nods. "Yeah."

The rest falls into place. "And you're the den mother. The one who keeps the edges safe when people choose to play."

He's ducking my gaze now, and he almost looks embarrassed. "Yeah. Something like that." His fingers trace over the lines of his tats. "I know what it is to need edges. And to need something in between."

I look at the strong, beautiful tribal lines of his ink. It's time to ask where he's trying to drive this thing, because if I don't want to be a passenger, I need to get off this bus really soon. I put my hands on the envelope. "So what's this?"

Chapter Eight

HARLAN

Subs pin me to the floor exactly never. Scorpio just has, and she's not even my sub yet.

I look at her and try to figure out the answer to a question that should be obvious, but somehow isn't. "It's an invitation."

She's staring me down just fine. "Scenes are about finding edges, right?"

Yeah. Especially when your Dom is a hard-ass, and I am. "Usually. Especially for the sub."

She takes a long, slow breath. "I think I come hang out here because you're all people who know what it is to seek out edges, to need to do that, and I like soaking that in. You feel like my tribe."

"You don't get enough of that other places."

She shrugs. "I get other things. Work makes me feel useful and needed, and they're my friends and they don't bleed every day, and I need that too."

I've been at her offices enough to know the adoration is mutual. They're as tight as we are, and I know exactly how rare that is. But the woman in front of me is still hungry. "But they aren't edge seekers."

She grins. "Well, Emily is surprising me."

She's surprising the whole damn universe. "She's doing it because she loves Damon." And Leo does it because he loves his partner, but I don't know how much Scorpio knows about that, so I keep my mouth shut.

Besides, this isn't about love. It's about helping someone who might belong in my lifestyle find her way there. I've got a really big comfort zone with that, even if this thing somehow keeps wobbling outside of it. I touch the envelope again. "This is edge. For sure. But it sounds to me like you want some of that in your life—you just want it balanced with some healthy stuff in between."

Her eyes are big, but she's nodding.

I take the leap. "I think we're the same on that. I'm in a lifestyle that defaults to edges, but part of my job is to hang out here and help make that in-between space, for me and for everyone else."

She's smiling. "Big scary Dom and den mother."

I give her a hard look. "You're totally going to ruin my street cred if you keep saying that shit." If she says it where Damon and Ari can hear, it's going to end up on a damn t-shirt. One that they try to make me wear.

Scorpio just smirks and sips her lemonade.

She's way more immune to my hard looks than a sub should be. I go back to the story I'm trying to tell. "You found yourself a life that has the warm and safe that you need, but it doesn't come with enough built-in edges, so you come hang out here when you need a hit."

She winces. "Yeah. Something like that. Or I go clubbing or bungee jumping or whatever."

I've been a Dom, and a good one, for fifteen years. And I'm in absolutely virgin territory right now. I tap the envelope again like it's my touchstone. "This is an invitation to the edges. But it's also an invitation to play with someone who shares your need for something good and strong and real in between those edges."

Her eyebrows slide up really slowly. "What does that mean?"

I have no fucking idea. "That you play with me and join this tribe instead of getting your high secondhand. And in between, we stay aware and figure it out and cobble together what works."

She's just plain staring now. "Like what?"

I feel the very unmanly need to babble. "Like you drop by with cookies or because you need a cuddle. And I drop by with a screwdriver to do stupid shit that doesn't need doing and get a hit of the sweet and light in your office and maybe you choose to be part of that sometimes."

She's grinning now, and I can see I've just said the right thing, even though I felt like a total idiot saying it.

Time to get this thing back to stuff I know how to do. I rip open the envelope, pull out a couple of pictures, and slap them onto the bar.

Scorpio glances at them. "No."

So much for floggers and high heels.

I pull out a few more, careful to position them this time so I can see her eyes.

She scans them, and then touches the middle one, smiling. "Punk-rock gear and fetish wear are pretty much the same thing."

I can teach her the error of that assumption later. One's designed to be a whole lot easier to take off. I lay more pictures down.

This time, her nose wrinkles. "Eww. No."

I look down at the photos, trying to figure out which one set her off. "Rope bondage?"

She shakes her head. "Maid costume."

That has my Dom radar going off big-time. "Why?"

Her eyes spark. "Do I need a reason?"

"No." I keep my voice away from the bossy end of things. I don't get to demand things of this woman—not yet. "But if you have one, I'd like to hear it."

"Sorry for biting your head off." She looks it. "The whole servant thing pushes a lot of buttons for me. Being treated as less. Not something I want to go anywhere near. Slave's even worse."

She's not going to like the next question, but it's my job to ask it. "Tricky territory that you might want to explore when there's enough trust in place, or hard limit?"

She flashes mad and then confused and then curious, rapidly enough I have to work to keep up. "How the hell do I tell that?"

I push the other two photos out of the way and leave the one of the woman in the seriously scanty maid costume. "When you look at this does it make you feel aroused and ashamed, or aroused and scared, or is it just a turn-off?"

"Turn-off." Her answer comes quick and sure.

I've walked countless newbie subs through trying to make sense of their own reactions. I fucking love how well she sees herself and how willing she is to look. "Okay. Then that sounds like a hard limit for you."

She's eyeing me. "And that's no big deal?"

I wink at her. "If your Dom's not an asshole—and he isn't."

She glares. "I haven't agreed to anything yet."

I let her last word hang in the air and pull out three more pictures. This time, I see the thing in her eyes I've been watching for. Softening. Yearning.

And then avoidance.

She pushes a woman in restraints my way and grins. "I like

this one."

I'm really good at my job because I can see all the reactions, not just the obvious ones. She's telling me the truth, but she's doing it to cover a truth she doesn't want me to see. I look down at the picture she's willing to talk about. A gorgeous woman in soft leather cuffs, tied to a headboard, a hairsbreadth away from orgasm. Eyes wide open and looking at her Dom.

Oh, yeah. I could work with that. Ari is a goddamn genius.

Scorpio's watching me, a little nervous and more than a little aroused. If she was my sub, I'd be sucking those gorgeous, hard nipples of hers as a reward for this gift she's just offered up. Since she's not, I have to content myself with words. "What do you see when you look at this?"

She runs her finger down the edge of the photograph. "Surrender that's not weak."

In four words, she's just defined the kind of sub she wants to be. The kind of sub she needs to be. And everything in me wants a chance to walk with her while she goes there.

She swallows, loud enough that I can hear her. "What do you see when you look at this?"

I wait until her eyes meet mine, until I know she'll keep them there. "A woman who is totally fucking sexy."

The air quivers between us. A choice on the line. And one that I know better than to force, no matter what the heat inside me wants.

I sweep all the photos back into the envelope. I haven't forgotten about the yearning eyes and whatever she's avoiding, but that needs to come after she decides. "Go away and follow the instructions this time."

She takes the envelope and looks at me with those big, serious eyes of hers. And then she slides off her stool and walks away.

Chapter Nine

SCORPIO

Emily peers down at her list and scrunches her nose in the way that tells the rest of us we're almost at the end and she's checking to see if anything new mysteriously added itself while we've been eating donuts and taking care of business.

Or at least Leo and I have been eating donuts. Gabby has this idea that she has too many curves and Meghan doesn't eat sugar and Emily's so high on Damon she probably doesn't eat anything anymore. Which means more donuts for me.

I lean forward and grab the last one in the box. It's vaguely person shaped, and when I bite off the head, it's full of blood. Probably raspberry filling, but I have to take my edges where I can find them these days.

Or at least that's what I thought right up until Harlan decided to get weird and shake things up. Now he's offering me a real edge to ride and I don't want it to fuck up my nice, safe, donut-laden life. Which makes me a wimp or something even sadder—but I've seen women sign on with a Dom, and none of them ever come out the same.

Including the obnoxiously cheerful one leading this meeting. I lean forward, suddenly restless and needing out of chair captivity. "So we have three new fall weddings, two of them at Fettered, and everything else is just follow-up, right?" Small steps forward on weddings that are months into the planning with months more to go. Apparently only the kinky folks are in a hurry.

Meghan drains the rest of her coffee. "We've got more referrals coming in from the BDSM community. The word's out that we're friendly."

Leo smirks. "The word's out that Emily can convince Damon to let a bunch of glitter and flowers and streamers loose in his club."

Emily somehow manages to keep looking professional. "Developing locations is part of my job."

Leo's flat out laughing now. "Is that what we're calling it?"

Clearly he's in on the pool to make her blush. I hand him the raspberry-blood-filled bottom half of my donut. "Back off, hot stuff. You're just jealous because she got spanked last night and you didn't."

Emily clears her throat, her prim face totally in place. "I'll have you know I got spanked this morning, thank you very much."

Meghan groans, Leo high-fives Emily, and Gabby turns as pink as her dress. I shake my head. Just another day at the office, or at least the new version of my office that got abducted by aliens and then sent back. Not that I mind. This is the kind of wedding-planning company that might actually hire somebody like me.

"One last thing." Emily cuts through the hilarity with amused eyes and the voice that makes her the nicest dictator on the planet. "Fettered has formally invited all of us to attend their charity ball at the end of the month. It's at a swanky hotel, with a romance theme, although that probably means something a little different than it would if we were in charge of decorating. Ari says to think evening gowns. Silk and satin and classy sex."

Leo grins. "I totally have an evening gown like that."

The paper airplane I throw at his head doesn't miss.

He throws it back and blows me a kiss. "Sam and I will be there."

Meghan's shaking her head. "I think I'll be taking that week off. We don't have any weddings, and I need a break."

Nobody points out that a charity ball isn't work. She isn't as easy with the energy of Fettered as the rest of us, and that needs to be okay. I like that nobody's pushing her. That's how edges start drawing blood.

"Well, um." Gabby looks shy, and more than a little flustered, but determined. "I think I'd like to go. If someone can help me figure out what to wear."

Leo's hand is in the air before she finishes her sentence.

I keep my hand down, because I shouldn't be dressing anyone, but I'm glad he's going to help. He'll make sure she doesn't show up looking like she wants to be gobbled. Although anyone who tries is probably going to have to run a gantlet of big, bad Doms. Gabby might not need a keeper, but she's got a shit-ton of volunteers.

Emily turns to me and raises an eyebrow. I nod, because of course I'll go. I'll have fun, even if I'll die before I slide this bod into an evening gown. But I'm also feeling sandpapered. This is an easy choice for me. Showing up to a Fettered dance might be Gabby's edge, but it's not mine. It's me hanging out on the sidelines again, inhaling someone else's smoke, just like I do when I watch grape farmers at weddings.

I'm a tourist in way too many lifestyles.

Leo moves to the chair beside me as the other three head out of the room. "So, who's the guy?"

I raise an eyebrow and put on the poker face that kept me solvent on way too many road trips. "Who says there's a guy?"

He snickers. "Okay, who's the girl?"

I roll my eyes. "Been there, tried that, got evicted from the island."

He picks up his laptop, stands up, and blows me a kiss. "Fine, don't share."

I can't, not yet. There's a guy I have to go talk to first.

Again.

Chapter Ten

HARLAN

I close the door behind me and finish locking up. I love being the last one out, putting the club to bed for the night and strolling home at an hour when pretty much everyone else is sleeping.

I can feel the chill in the wind on my cheeks. The first touches of winter, or what passes for it here in Seattle, anyhow. I grin at the door handle. Standing here thinking poetic shit in the middle of the night is a sure sign I need to get laid.

"Hey."

The voice behind me activates every nerve I have, and that's before I register that it's Scorpio and not some thug who wants to crack me over the head and steal my wallet. Some really high, blind, stupid thug. Nobody even a little bit sane tries to rob a guy with as much ink and muscle as I have.

I apparently don't scare the woman leaning against the tree, though. "It's not smart to walk the streets alone at night."

She's got her poker face on. "I don't need a protector."

I need to be one, but that's a fight we can have later. I'm way more interested in why she's here. "How long have you been out here?" We have club hours, but respect for those hours is a totally different thing—and the middle-of-the-night time is my favorite. Scenes are done, newbies have gone home, and I get to take off my manager hat and enjoy the people who are the core of my world.

"Not long." Scorpio hasn't moved from her tree. "Want to take a walk?"

"Yeah." I punch the final codes into the door alarm system and hold out my hand. "Which way do you live? I'll walk you home."

She studies my hand for a minute and then offers me hers. I hold my breath as our fingers slide together, feeling her skin on mine, the dance as our energies get to know each other a little.

"You do this with all the subs you're chasing?" She's still staring at our hands.

"No." I shrug and tell her the truth. "With friends, mostly." Touch is a permission thing in my world, so it's something I'm careful with, even though I'm a guy who drinks it up like water.

She looks at me. "This feels different than friends."

"Yeah." I tug her gently toward the street. "Is that why you're here?"

"Maybe." She points with her free hand. "I live that way."

Conveniently, so do I. We walk together quietly. I listen to the sound of our footsteps, feel the warmth flowing from her hand to mine. In the vanilla world, holding hands doesn't mean much. In mine, it's a big deal.

She pats the bag hanging over her shoulder. "I picked some images."

Tension zings through me and straight into our joined hands. I made my instructions very clear. If all she wants to play is beta tester, she'd be having this conversation with Ari. I stop us on the sidewalk and back up until I can lean against a low stone wall so that my eyes are level with hers. I need to be really sure what she's chosen. "You're bringing them to me. You want us to play with whatever you've picked."

She stares at me and nods.

The lessons start right now. "Words. You want this, you need to own it out loud where we can both hear it."

She reaches into her bag and draws out a manila envelope. This one's a pretty green color and a lot skinnier than the one I gave her. She puts it on the stone wall beside me. "Those are the ones I picked." She swallows. "I think I'm a sub, and I think this is what I want. But I'm going to be really honest and say that I know a lot of people who want to sing behind a microphone in their daydreams, but they crap out fast when they actually try it."

Somewhere in that bare-naked honesty she's stopped meeting my eyes. I reach for her chin. "That's what safewords are for. I take care of my subs, Scorpio—even if that means stopping dead in our tracks and curling up in a chair for as long as it takes until you feel okay again."

She nods slowly, and her eyes are full of the kind of courage that only happens when you know you might fail and want to try anyhow.

"If we do this, I'll push you like hell, because that's part of the deal for me. But all it will ever take for you to push back is one really small word, even if you said yes to that thing two seconds earlier."

She eyes me wryly. "You're very good at this, aren't you?"

I want to touch so much more than her hand. "Playing's no fun if you have to get it right every time. We'll explore, we'll try some things, we'll talk, we'll try some more things." I hold up our linked hands. "So since we've already tried something— is this okay?"

Her smile is softer than usual. "Yeah."

"Good." I put my free hand on her envelope. "What about you sitting in my lap while we look at these together?"

"Ah—" I can hear the disconcerted surprise in her voice. And the arousal.

God she's hot. "Or we can go find a bench somewhere and sit without touching, and talk pictures and contracts."

She's eyeing me. "You do contracts? Even when it's not a club thing?"

I shrug. "For myself, I mostly just need a good, clear conversation, but Fettered requires paperwork for lots of smart reasons, so I stick with that just to keep everything clean. You okay with that?"

She's nodding. "Yeah. But I don't want that vibe when we're checking out the porn."

I like her style. "Porn first. Lap or bench?"

I can see the shaky breath she pulls in. "Lap."

My cock is fully in favor of this plan, which she's about to find out. I reach for her other hand and pull her in between my legs. "What's your safeword, Scorpio?"

She stares at me, and I can feel her wanting to lean in. To connect. To soak in what I'm putting out there for her.

Damn. This is going to be freaking combustible. I squeeze her hands. "Safeword. Something really easy for you to remember."

She swallows hard. "Lightning."

I grin. "I like that one. Where's it from?"

She laughs quietly. "It's the name of my favorite electric guitar."

She's made it personal, which is smart. And told me why, which is the kind of naked and honest I need and want from her. And she's waiting for my signal to move, even though everything in her wants to cuddle in.

She's not wrong about being a sub.

I let my Dom have a few inches of leash. He and I both need to remember that I don't have permission for squat yet. I let go of her hands long enough to scoop her up, one arm reaching behind her back, the other lifting at her knees. I set her down sideways on my lap, which makes my legs and my erection and the chest she's cuddling into like she belongs there all very happy.

I breathe for a moment. It's one of the best things I ever learned as a Dom. Pause. Be in the damn moment. I won't be holding Scorpio for the first time ever again, and every inch of her is hot and sweet and mine and right where I want her.

She's got her nose practically buried in my chest. I know what she's doing, because I'm smelling her too. Imprinting on her scent. Autumn leaves and salt and something that smells totally lickable.

Then I feel her shiver, and I realize we don't have all night, because eventually we'll freeze to death on this stone wall. I reach for her envelope and lay it in her lap. "Show me what you want, beautiful."

Her hands are shaking, and I slide one of mine under her jacket to the small of her back. Steadying. Giving her an anchor. We've suddenly gone way deeper than I expected, and we're not nearly done yet.

We both need me to be her Dom right now. The words will catch up.

Chapter Eleven

SCORPIO

I am falling into this man and all I'm doing is sitting in his lap. I'm pretty sure that's dangerous, but nothing in me wants to move.

His head slides down by my ear. "Show me." His voice is full of gravel, and it has my hands jumping to obey.

It doesn't do shit for steadying them, however. When I picked out the photos I liked from the comfort of my own couch, it felt like a game. This doesn't feel like a game at all. I'm acutely aware that if I show this man what's in this envelope, he's going to do those things to me. Not as his partner, his equal, his sexy playmate.

As his sub.

I know what surrender is—I've let myself go into more songs and pounding beats than I can count. And I know that Harlan won't stand for anything less.

I somehow manage to get the envelope open and dump the photos onto my lap. "I only picked three." My words sound all wispy and apologetic, and that pisses me off. I lean into his hand on my back. "There's more I liked, but these are the ones that jumped out at me strongest. I think that's what you wanted."

He puts a hand over the pictures, blocking his view. "Tell me what I'm going to see."

I don't want to be naked that fast. "You have eyes. Use them."

"Mouthy sub." He sounds amused. "Remind me that we need to spend extra time on the punishment clause in the contract."

I can't resist. "You could sing to me. That would probably cover it." Ari brought him to karaoke night once. The man has many talents. Tolerable pitch isn't one of them.

His hand tangles in my hair and pulls, hard enough to get my attention. "Brat."

I tip my head back and look straight into his eyes. "If that's not what you want to sign up for, say so before I totally embarrass myself here. I don't put myself in the closet of girls with good manners for anyone."

I love the smile that sneaks onto his face. "Yeah. Got that."

It sounds like he maybe does. "How does that work with being your sub?"

This smile is long, slow, and deadly. "Only one way to find out, beautiful."

He's undoing me, one gravelly word at a time. I sit up straight and look at dark shadows off in the distance. "One of the pictures is a room done in velvet. It's sexy, but not frilly or soft. Another is the restraints one you already saw. The last one is—" I glare at him. "It would be easier to just get naked."

His eyes are eating me up. "Welcome to my world. What's the last photo?"

"He's undressing her." I fire the words out, trying to push him back with them. "She's just standing there."

He lifts his hand up, and his voice is back to gravel. "Show me."

I manage to find that image without dropping the others, which, given how badly my hands are shaking, is ridiculously hard.

He wraps his hand around mine, and I can see his eyes studying the picture. I've told him the basics, but they're not what matters. A woman is standing in soft light, her head tipped back on the shoulder of the man behind her. She's dressed in underwear we can't really see and what is probably his shirt, and he's sliding the shirt off one shoulder. All body parts are covered. It's practically chaste.

Except for the look on her face.

I freaking hope he doesn't see that part. "I'm assuming he keeps going after the shirt."

His chest rumbles around me. "Duh."

I squiggle a little further away on his lap. His hard cock against my leg I can handle. It's the rest of the intimacy of this that's freaking me out. "So, I picked. I showed you. What now?"

His fingers are lifting my chin again. "Next is the contract. And know that after you sign it, this avoidance crap stops. You think something, you feel something—you tell me."

I can feel myself crackling. "You don't own me."

"Wrong verb. Right idea." He's not backing down an inch. "You're new, but you're not that new. You know what a sub is. What she gives."

Edges. Fuck. "Fine. Let's do the contract."

He doesn't bother hiding his grin at all. "You're sexy when you're steamed, do you know that?"

I roll my eyes. "Get used to it. I have a feeling you're going to piss me off a lot."

He's still laughing as he pulls a small tablet out of a pocket in his jacket. "You okay with squinting at a small screen? If not I can email this to you and we can do it in the morning."

By then I might lose my nerve. "My eyes are young and limber. Is it the newbie contract? I've seen that one."

"Yeah." He thumbs his tablet a few times and hands it to me, and then slides me off his lap and onto the rock wall.

I know what he's doing. A different vibe for the contract than for the porn—just like I asked. He listened, and he's delivering, and that loosens something that's been tightening in my gut.

I make it through the first pages fast. He's right—I know what I'm signing up for. I'm a tourist who's read the guide-books. I slow down when I get to the possible areas of play. I've been involved in enough discussions on the couches at Fettered to have a pretty good idea of what I do and don't want to do, at least in theory. I mark a bunch off as hard and soft limits, green-light some of the others, and hand him the tablet. "Any questions?"

He glances at me as he takes it. "That's usually my line."

I shrug. "I'm not much for paperwork. Words matter."

He hands it back. "Any of your green-light stuff less than enthusiastic?"

I shake my head. "Nope." I've heard Ari's speech on that a hundred times, even though it wasn't ever pointed at me. "Anything at all uncertain I've put in soft limits for now. There are a lot of those, but I'm okay with trying them."

"We will."

I thumb through to what I know is the hard stuff, and screw up my face at the first lines. "Punishment clause." I put down the tablet and look at him.

His smile is pure sin. "We're going to need one."

I sigh, and then try to stumble through the mess of my own insides. "This is one of those arousing, but also disturbing, areas for me. I know sometimes punishment is mostly a play thing and the subs are angling for it. Emily does that a lot." Which seems to surprise everyone, including her.

Harlan grins. "Yes, she does."

"So that kind of stuff, that's all good. I know I have a mouth, and I suspect we could have fun playing with that." I pause, but he's silent, waiting for me to finish. "But I don't like the idea of you using punishment to shut down who I am."

He's quiet, and I can tell he's really thinking. "That's not what it's about, at least not for me. If you're sassing me to play with me, to bring all of who you are into the scene, then that works. But if it's getting in the way of your surrender—if you're using it as cover or as a defense or as a way to try to top from the bottom in a non-playful way—then that's a problem and I will be shutting that right the fuck down."

I blink. "Wow. You don't mince words."

"Nope. I don't. Does that work for you?"

He's telling me he's going to keep me riding the sharp part of the edges whether I like it or not.

But he's also said he'll be there to catch me once we get off. I need to hear him say it again. "If you have to push on me like that, I'm going to be a mess after."

He reaches forward and strokes his knuckle down my cheek. "That's part of it too. I won't drop you. That's my end of the deal. You don't have to walk any of this by yourself, and if you can't stand my face, then Ari or Damon or Emily or Leo or Quint will take care of you."

I blow out my breath into the cold night, missing his lap and wanting to get this done. "Okay. I can work with that."

Chapter Twelve

HARLAN

She's running out of gas. She's totally shown up for this, and if I were a nice Dom, I'd stop now and let her think about things and get some sleep and talk to me in the morning.

I'm not nice.

I pick up the tablet and scroll back to make sure I have her selections locked in my mind. "There's one thing I need us to talk about a little more." I point my finger at a bullet that matters a lot to me. "Public scening. You have it as a soft limit, but I want to dig into some more specifics around that. What are you up for, at least in theory?"

Her face screws up in a way I'm already finding intolerably cute. "You mean public like at the club?"

Time to see just how comfortable with all this she really is. "There too, but also outside." I trail a finger up the side of her jeans, because I plain can't keep my hands off her anymore. "Like if I wanted to pull you back into my lap right now and slide my fingers into your jeans and make you come."

She's staring at me and her breath is coming in jerking pants. Part of me is freaking turned on, and part of me is scared she's going to say no to something it would truly hurt me to give up. I try to keep both things dialed down as much as I can. She needs to choose without my reactions leaning all over her.

She's pulling herself back under control. "I don't think I want anyone else to see. Not up close, anyhow. That feels like a hard limit."

I need to know its exact contours, because this is my favorite damn playground, and at least some of it clearly turns her on. "Would it be okay if people were suspicious about what we were doing? Like if somebody came out on that balcony over there and watched you wiggling on my lap while my hand was down your pants?"

If she squirms any harder, she's going to come right on top of our rock wall. "I think that's okay."

Damn, I like her. She's letting me push, letting herself feel into the pushing and giving me truth. There's nothing sexier, and my need to bend her over and fuck her in the middle of a Seattle street is getting outrageous.

The fact that she hasn't totally ruled that out for someday in the future is driving me even crazier. "How about if people can hear us? Hear you?" I lower my voice. "If they can hear my hand spanking your ass, or if I order you to be as loud as you want to be and people can hear you moan and scream as you come?"

I can see her cheeks going red, even in the dark, and I want to be absolutely sure I know why. "This is one of my favorite kinks, beautiful. If it turns you on that's nothing to be ashamed of."

She lets out a whoosh of a breath. "I'm not ashamed. A little embarrassed, yeah, and a lot turned on, so I'm not thinking very straight." She chews her lip. "I was a singer for a long time. A performer. I like having an audience. I can maybe see liking that here too. Not in close, but letting other people connect to that energy, putting it out there in the world instead of hiding it away in a bedroom somewhere."

She's just put something into words that I've known my whole adult life and never been able to explain. It's never been about people watching me. It's been about not hiding. About sharing. About the energies of sex and passion and control and surrender being so wildly messed up in the world and about putting some drops back into that ocean that don't buy into all the bullshit.

Scorpio's watching me intently. She holds up a hand. A caution—a gentle one. "I don't know for sure. This feels like one of those things I could totally change my mind on without a lot of warning."

If she does, I'll stop. But I've been at this gig long enough that I don't think she's going to. Not when she has such a deep connection to why. BDSM is a head game more than anything else. I point my finger at the contract. "Almost done. Open contract or closed?"

She raises an eyebrow, takes the tablet back, and reads the fine print.

I know what it says. I also know what I want this time— and I'm surprising myself.

She looks up. "Okay, so there's two parts. I'm fine with open time limits. We end it when at least one of us is done."

That's the easy part. "Agreed. What about other people? Open or closed?"

She wrinkles her face. "I know what people think about musicians, and they're not wrong, but I'm pretty much a serial monogamist. One guy at a time. I might be willing to try stretching that if it's important to you, but that's my starting place."

She deserves honesty from her Dom. "I usually do open. It's not what I want this time."

I see the surprise flare in her eyes, and it's beautiful. I plan to keep surprising her. After we make damn sure all the details are clear. "That can only apply to actual scenes and sexual contact with others, though. My job involves lots of watching other people and stepping in when I need to, which can include things like cuddling a half-naked sub in my lap while she cries."

She smiles and taps her finger on my tablet. "Okay. Closed to other people, with the caveat that Scorpio is a big girl and knows that Harlan has a job to do."

Damn. My arousal hasn't gone anywhere, but I'm also discovering layers of this woman I really like that are way beyond than the visceral ones. I reach over and swipe through to the signature page. "You can think about it if you want."

She's already working through the electronic signature protocol. "Already did that before I showed up with porn and sat in your lap."

I grin—she's pretty damn irresistible. "That was a big highlight in my day."

She looks up, and all I can see is the flaring desire in her eyes. "Yeah. Mine too."

Chapter Thirteen

SCORPIO

He has his hands on me and my ass back in his lap faster than I can take my next breath.

I shiver, and it has nothing to do with being cold. "What are you doing?"

He takes the tablet out of my hands and slides it into his bag. "You signed. You're mine. Be at the club at noon tomorrow. Don't touch yourself tonight."

He has to be freaking kidding me. The heat between my legs is going to turn me into human gelatin soon. "Are you always going to be this mean?"

He tips his head down into my neck and bites. "Yes. But I also have a one-time offer for you." His hand slides to the waistband of my jeans. "My fingers in your pussy, right now. You come fast and you come hard and you come loud and you don't give a damn if half the neighborhood leans out their windows to watch."

It's three a.m. and they're all dead asleep, but the idea of them watching floods my panties anyhow. "Yes. Go."

He bites my neck again, and his fingers are already working my belt loose. "What's your safeword?"

"Lightning." I gasp as his hand heads into the back of my jeans, his middle finger running down the cleft of my ass. It's a tight fit, and every inch he slides further down has my clit sitting up and begging. I squish my face into his chest and moan.

He squeezes my ass, and his finger is so damn close to where I need it to be. "Louder. I want them to hear you."

Louder isn't hard. I have singer lungs, and I've never been quiet. This time I moan out into the night, and I can feel how hard it makes him under my leg.

Then his other hand reaches to undo the snap and zipper of my jeans. He lifts me up a couple of inches like I weigh absolutely nothing, and then he's got both hands down my pants, one holding my ass and the other sliding fingers into my hot, wet, begging pussy.

"Fuck." He makes the word sound sacred. "You're soaked."

I sink into his fingers. Way too many guys treat my parts like fine china. "Don't be gentle."

His back hand clamps on my ass and he's got two fingers up inside me before I can even suck in a breath.

This time the sound I make is a lot closer to a whimper. "God. Please."

He curls his fingers against my G-spot and starts a fast, hard drumbeat. He's lit a fire, and his fingers are the fuel and the oxygen and I'm about to be engulfed by the flames that are already starting to ripple.

My thighs fight for micro-movements, rocking in his hands, begging for the explosion that's so close I can feel it threatening in every cell.

His head is back in the crook of my neck. "I want to feel you come in my hand, beautiful."

I tilt my head back and let loose a single, guttural cry and squirt wet, messy, desperate release all over his fingers, and then I keep rocking, because one wasn't nearly enough to shut down this wildfire he's lit inside me.

He growls into the top of my head. "Stop. I didn't say you could have more than one." His fingers slide out of me, but he cups my pussy as his other hand strokes up my back and cuddles me into his chest. "I want you lying in bed tonight, thinking of my hands on you and making frustrated noises as you lie there and can't sleep."

His fingers are still playing with my pussy in a way that's making me crazy but isn't going to make me come. "I hate you."

His laughter rumbles against my ear. "I kind of hate me right now too."

Given the rod of iron I can feel against my leg, I can only imagine. "Please tell me there are stupid rules for you too and you don't get to go home and jerk off in the shower."

"I get to do whatever I need to do to have my head screwed on straight as your Dom."

I blink. I'm already figuring out that he can snap into that arrogant Dom space fast enough to give me whiplash.

He slides his wet hand out of my pants and runs it slowly up my belly and cups my breast. The hand on my back is still gently stroking. Petting. It feels totally cuddly, with undemanding, erotic low notes. I curl in closer. "So, I'm pretty touchy-feely. Especially after. Is that the kind of thing I should be telling you?"

"Yes." I can feel him smiling into the top of my head. "Even when it's really obvious."

He doesn't seem at all upset, but it's been a thing a few times in my past. "That a problem?"

His hands go still on me, as if he can see the tricky spot I'm trying to go around. "You know what aftercare is?"

"I've seen it in action at the club, but it always seems kind

of perfunctory. A hug, a bottle of water, and everyone's good."
I know I'm needier than that.

He's quiet. "That's good to know, actually. You've mostly
seen scenes at our open nights, and those are usually pretty
tame and done by really experienced members."

The lightbulb is going off. "So they don't need much in the
way of aftercare."

"Yeah, exactly." He's stroking my hair now. "For private or
more intense scenes, the aftercare piece can easily stretch into
hours. It usually does with me anyhow. I'm a big fan of an
armful of naked woman."

He's soothing something in me that I didn't even expect
him to understand.

He pulls me in closer, like we have all the time in the world
to cuddle on a rock wall in the middle of a cold fall night.
"Plan to stay most of tomorrow. The room we'll be using has a
really big, squishy bed. I'll hold you after we scene for as long
as you want, including sleep if you like."

I raise an eyebrow, because I can still feel his erection
pulsing against me. "Hold me, huh? You must have some
pretty fancy self-control."

I can hear his amusement again. "I haven't bent you over
this wall and fucked you until neither of us can stand, so yeah,
my self-control is pretty good."

I groan as the sticky mess between my legs gets wet and
slick again.

He runs a hand down my belly and into my heat and starts
to chuckle. "I like the way you think, beautiful." His other
hand pats my ass. "Stand up. Let's get you home."

I stand where he puts me, legs quaking as he zips up my
jeans and does up my belt, and I wonder what the heck I've
gotten myself into.

Because whatever I might have imagined over the years? It wasn't this.

Chapter Fourteen

HARLAN

Someday I'll get smart.

I look at the private room I've picked for my first scene with Scorpio, knowing I'm way more tired than I should be—and knowing not much is going to change until I have my way with every damn inch of her.

I lift up the hand that got to spend time in her pussy last night. I've had a shower, but my nose is convinced that my fingers still smell like her. I don't know what else today might bring, but I'm damn sure I'm going to spend some time fondling her slick, wet heat. And watching her face this time, because the photos she chose told me about more than some of the kinks she finds interesting.

Scorpio wants her Dom to be watching.

Not that I plan to be doing anything else, but it's good to know what tools I've got to play with.

I look around the room, damn happy with Ari. She's our interior decorator, and Scorpio's not the only one who thinks velvet is sexy. Ari calls this room rich bordello, but it's classier than that. Leather floors, which I didn't even know were a thing, some kind of textured stuff on the walls that reminds me of the dojo I hung out in as a teenager, and a bed that's all velvet and silk and sin. She's nailed the lighting, too—not too bright, but angled so that very little in here will happen in shadows.

Scorpio wants her Dom to be watching.

I sigh as my cock gets hard. "She's not even here yet. Get a grip."

He doesn't listen very well.

I've brought in what I need in addition to the basics. I traded out Milo's newest creation for one of my old favorites. This one's his too, but it's got a lot less bells and whistles. Just a bench with some sexy curves and padding in all the right places and a restraint system that Fettered's subs swear is the best thing going.

I make it my business to listen to the people who actually get tied up.

I double-check the cuffs I've chosen—wide, padded, and covered in the softest leather we have. Good newbie restraints. They'll give Scorpio something to hold on to, something to fight against while she learns what it really means to give herself to me.

I pull and tug on attachment points, checking the adjustability that Milo is famous for, knowing I'm wasting my time. His gear rarely breaks, and our experienced subs speak up at the slightest creak or wobble.

I reach under the bench for my basket of toys. Scorpio's pictures didn't give me much help on what she's hoping for after the clothes come off and the cuffs go on. Which is fine with me, because I'm a Dom, not a fantasy man-puppet.

I roll my eyes as I lift out the baby flogger that wasn't there when I tucked the basket away. Apparently Ari has left us a present. It's not a bad one—the flogger is small enough and soft enough to be safe even in the hands of the most inexperienced Dom, and in the hands of a good one, it's a very effective tease.

I check to make sure our resident practical joker hasn't left any other surprises, and then I tuck everything away under the velvet slipcover that puddles to the ground, making the bench look like nothing more than a luxurious place to lay out and take a nap.

I'm so ready. Where the fuck is my sub?

Chapter Fifteen
SCORPIO

I march into Fettered like I own the place, which isn't hard because the front door's wide open and there's music blaring loud enough to cover the sounds of a dozen women stomping around in their army boots.

I swear, if I only get one orgasm today, Harlan is a dead man walking.

I peer into the darkness of the lounge and don't see anything except for a chalkboard sign sitting prominently on the end of the bar where I can't possibly miss it, covered in Ari's distinctive, stylish handwriting. *He's back in the private rooms, last door on your left. It's the only one that will be open. Good luck, and don't do anything I wouldn't do.*

I snort, even though nerves have just entirely, thoroughly landed. I pick up the piece of chalk she left conveniently at the bottom and scrawl a note. *I need a list of what those things are.* Then I grin to myself, because I can already hear her laughter.

Which seems like the right way to pay her back for making sure I feel loved this morning.

I dust the chalk off my hands and continue the walk that

started in the dark hours of last night and left me restless and wanting and totally sleepless in my own bed. The music fades as I swing through the doors into the dungeon. It looks a bit strange, empty of people and full of sunlight. I don't look too hard at the equipment, but I do see a set of tools lying out and a sprawl of lug nuts laid out beside one of the chairs.

A repair in progress. Somebody got themselves out of the way so I would do this walk alone. I swallow and wonder just how many people know what's about to happen. My Dom, making a statement.

My Dom. Holy fucking hell.

I shake my head and snap my shoulders straight. He didn't exactly do me wrong last night, and I have at least some idea of what's going to happen in this room. Which might not actually be making things any easier. My frustrated nocturnal fantasies were full of cuffs and velvet and strong, talented hands stripping me naked.

At this rate I'm going to come before he touches me.

I get to the door on the other side of the dungeon. The one I've never passed through, the threshold I've never crossed. What lies beyond is member-only territory, and only after they've jumped through a bunch of hoops, because Fettered is obnoxiously careful with their people.

I'm getting a pass on all of that because the man who's waiting for me is Dom gold.

My legs are the kind of jittery they were for my first really big gigs, and I know that if I don't get moving I'm in big trouble. I push through the doors and find myself in a hallway that could belong to a classy hotel. The doors have discreet signs, but I don't stop to read them. I can see the one that's open, and it has my full attention.

I don't feel myself walking anymore. I only see the room

widening in front of me as I get closer. Rich brown floor and rice-paper walls and a smell that's straight out of a fantasy I didn't even know I had. And the bed. I stop just inside the doorway, gaping at it. It takes up half the room, a maroon-and-chocolate paradise covered in silk and velvet and something that might be fake fur of the really spectacular kind.

I want to peel off all my clothes and dive in.

And then I feel the breath at my neck. The hands closing on my upper arms to stop my instinctive spin. The heat of the man right behind me, but not quite touching.

My entire body quivers.

A low chuckle at my neck. "You like?"

I'm not sure what he's asking about, but I like it all. "Is it bad to say I want to live in that bed?"

His hands lift off my arms, and all I have holding me up is his breath. "That can happen. After."

I'm losing track of his words. Everything in me is focused on the back of my neck.

A finger touches, feather light, just below my ear and traces down to my collarbone. "How'd you sleep?"

I moan, putting every bit of nine hours of frustration into the sound.

He closes the inch between my back and his front, and suddenly I'm enveloped in the energy of aroused male. One arm wraps around my waist, pulling me in tight, and the other one tweaks my nipple hard enough to hurt—and to drive a thrum of sensation right down to my toes.

This time the sound I make is entirely desperate.

His hold gentles. "I'm going to strip you naked, right here, so that I can see your beautiful breasts and every inch of this sexy skin. I'm going to torment you today, Scorpio, and these nipples of yours are right at the top of my list."

He's playing with the one he just tweaked, and the other one is dying for his touch. I reach up to move his hand.

He growls. "I touch what I want, and only what I want. You take what I give."

The gravel is back, and even though his words totally piss me off, they also make me whimper.

Chapter Sixteen

HARLAN

I have an armful of temperamental, seething, wildly aroused sub, and I'm pretty sure I've never been happier in my life.

Or harder.

My cock is going to totally hate me for this day.

I slide the shirt she's wearing off a shoulder and bite the skin I see. She jumps in my arms, and then soothes as I run my tongue over her skin. She's so damn soft, and she tastes vaguely of salt and spice. I contemplate the layers she's wearing and decide I'm too damn impatient for all of this to go slowly. I pull the loose shirt up over her head in one swift move. She sways on one shocked intake of breath and I catch her, my hands wrapping around her forearms.

I'm happy to do it. I want her unsteady. I slide one hand around to her belly. The other travels down her spine, annoyed by the tank top that covers way too much skin.

My sub wasn't looking to make this easy.

I peel this one up more slowly, keeping my attention on the small muscles of her back, the ripples as she takes small, panting breaths.

I can already smell the arousal on her skin. I pull her

against my chest and run both hands up under the tank to cup her breasts. They're soft and luscious and if all I got to do for the rest of the day was stand here and hold her like this, it would be a day worth having.

Her whimper snaps me back into gear. Her legs are shaking, enough that she's leaning back on me, looking for help staying on her feet.

I know what I've got in my hands. I need to know if she knows. I lean my head down to the side of her neck and take a lick because I can't freaking resist. "Scared?"

"No." Her breath hitches in, begging for my touch. "Drowning."

Good. I want her going under. I reach my hands for the nipples that have been taunting me for days and give them a firm squeeze. Dom pride lands hard at the cry that shoots out of her. I slide the tank top up and over her head. "I want to see, beautiful." I run my hands over her newly naked skin, shaping her into my chest, dropping her head back to my shoulder.

And feel her steadying.

That isn't something I'm going to let happen. Not when I'm chasing her surrender. I drag my finger slowly along her waistband. "I'm going to watch you as you come for me."

She's almost there, just on my words.

I start working her nipples again, first one, then the other. Giving her rhythm. Learning just how much pressure she likes, how much speed. Where the line is between what she thinks she wants and what she needs.

She's writhing against me—but not to get away. She's pushing back with her ass so that she can arch into my hands, and my cock is fucking slayed that I'm not going to let him out of captivity. I keep up the relentless pace of my hands. At this point I don't know if I'm doing this for her or for me, because watching her nipples get all rosy under my fingers is sweet damn torture.

I can hear how close she is. How much she needs this. How totally lost she is in my touch. I clamp my fingers on both nipples and roll them hard and she shoots over like I've launched her out of a cannon. The music she makes as she goes hits me deep where I live as a Dom.

I hold her against me, melding her body against mine, stroking her gently until her bones start remembering where they live. I circle a finger around one of her nipples, then the other, then a swooping spiral down to her pants. Same baggy jeans as yesterday, and after I undo her belt it only takes a heartbeat and a quick lift to step her out of them.

She's putty, but she's aware putty now. Coming back to me. Ready for more.

Good, because I'm not nearly ready to be done.

I run my hand under the sexy purple lace of her underwear and cup her heat. I just hold there. The next time I tip her over that edge, I want her lying down. This is just the in-between. A time for her to feel me holding her, to listen to my breath, to come back into hers. Her heart is beating into both of my hands, and it's outrageously sexy.

I wait until it slows, and then trace a finger over the edges of her lace panties. "See the curvy bench over there? Go lie down on that, on your back."

It takes a moment for the words to register. She lifts her head off my shoulder and glances over at the bed, clearly confused. "Why aren't we using that?"

Today I'll give her a little latitude with the questions. "More freedom of movement for me. Less for you."

Her eyes widen.

I let go of her and walk over to the bench. "Stop talking. Come lie down."

She manages to make it to the bench without her legs giving out, and collapses automatically onto her back, her eyes pinned to mine. I stroke a hand down her breast, over her belly. "Good girl."

Her whimpers are killing me.

I slide her up a little, so that she's got her head on the pillowed incline. Just enough tilt to make it easy for her to watch. "Hands up by your ears."

She's less sure what's going on now, and that's good. We're heading off her script and onto mine. I guide her hand into one of the leather cuffs that are positioned just above her ears. Milo's genius magnetic attachments—they hold like steel and everything releases with a single flip of a switch.

All Scorpio needs to know is that I'm shutting down her wiggle room.

I tighten the cuff slowly around her wrist. This is one of the places where sub rubber hits the road, and if she's got triggers around being restrained, we'll find out now. I keep my eyes on her face, on the throbbing pulse in her neck, on her nipples. The cuff tightens on a small intake of her breath, nothing more.

I move around to the other side, keeping everything slow. This time she moves her arm to help me, so I get this cuff on faster. She tugs against them and then freezes, her eyes shooting to mine.

My sub is learning. "Go ahead. See how they feel."

She doesn't mess around. A couple of good sharp tugs, and then a small smile.

Oh, yeah. This is going to be combustible.

I stroke a hand down her body again, just because I can, and slide the lacy scrap of purple off while I'm at it. Then I reach for her knees, bending them up and opening them. I hear myself growling as I drink in the sight of her wide open for me. I brush two fingers through her wetness. "My fingers smelled like you all damn night."

She jerks hard against the arm restraints.

I grin and slide my hands down her legs all the way to the ankles. I push the magic buttons that add a couple of new curves to the sides of the bench to support her legs. I make sure they're bent and open to give me all the access that I want, and then I slide on the ankle cuffs. Scorpio can see these going on, and the small, panting sounds she's making are going straight to my cock.

He has no idea how bad this day's going to get for him.

"Legs comfortable?" I wait for her nod, and then I pull up the wide, buttery leather straps that go around her legs and situate them mid-thigh. This is a lot of restraint for a beginner, but all her cues say she can do this. I keep watching her eyes as I put them on. She's surprised, but not scared.

Good. I don't think fear is her edge.

Immobility might be.

I make the last minor adjustments, using every damn bit of Milo's ingenuity to make my sub comfortable. Then I lay a hand on her knee. "If anything feels painful or uncomfortable or you get a cramp, you need to let me know right away."

She nods. "Yes, Sir."

Damn. That's not something I ever ask for from a sub, but I like hearing it from this one.

I stroke her, using my hands to let her know she's pleased me. Her eyes haze.

I grin and reach under the bench. We've covered the three photos she brought me. Now it's time to see how she rolls with a Dom who wants to know every damn thing about what turns her on.

Chapter Seventeen

SCORPIO

I have just enough time to see the thing in his hand. It looks like black spaghetti—or like a flogger someone shrank in the wash.

And then he flicks his wrist and black spaghetti reaches for my skin.

Hot rain.

That's all I have time to think, and then there's more of it falling and my skin is on fire with sensation. Tracing the sides of my body, up my outer thighs and over my hips and circling back down again. Each time he makes the trip around, the circle gets wider. Edging toward my breasts, over my belly, raining on the insanely sensitive skin of my inner thighs.

And I can't freaking move at all. I can feel myself trying to thrash, trying to move out of the hot rain, trying to move into it, desperate for wherever this is trying to take me. It goes on for seconds, for hours, for long enough that time folds and I have no idea where I am anymore.

Sensation. Kissing my skin, lashing it, becoming it.

It's not orgasm—that isn't the mountain we're climbing.

He's circling my breasts now, in a taunting figure-eight that knows exactly where it's headed. I close my eyes, unable to watch the craziness of my nipples reaching for the rain.

I hear the sound, the one that I somehow know is the flick of the black spaghetti in his hand, coming for me again. It lashes over my right breast, and for one crazy moment I almost can't stand it. And then his hand is there. Gentling. Steadying. Reminding me who controls the rain and who can make it go away.

His thumb strokes my cheek. "Open your eyes, beautiful."

I struggle to make my eyelids work. They feel cast in concrete. The first thing I see when I finally get them open is his face, looking at me like I'm the most gorgeous thing he's ever seen.

He trails the soft strings of leather across my nipples. Stroking this time. "Keep your eyes open for me."

The almost inaudible snapping sound, and the rain is falling again. On my belly this time, and then a slow, inexorable march up my ribs. It's not as sharp anymore—more like a heat that's swelling all over my body.

Harlan reaches for one of my nipples, rolling it in his fingers as he rains down fire on the other.

I'm so far beyond orgasm it's not even funny. I'm somewhere else, and I'm drinking hot rain with every pore I have.

He growls, a sound full of approval and pride and heat that lands right behind the rain and soaks into every inch of my skin. The lashes are coming faster now, the skin that hasn't felt them desperate and parched and begging.

If I could move, I'd show him where.

And then it stops, black spaghetti falling silent on my belly. I stare at it, bereft.

The low chuckle beside me yanks my eyes to his face. Harlan stands there, grinning at me like an idiot for a moment that lasts way too long, and then his hands are stroking me. Touching all the places the rain fell and all the places it didn't. Soothing.

Reminding me that there are things that are even better than hot rain.

Chapter Eighteen

HARLAN

I slide the baby flogger off of Scorpio's belly and realize I might have a new favorite toy. Sharpness without pain. Sensation without having to control every damn movement so precisely that I sometimes have to remind myself to breathe. A wave that my sub rode hard and furious and deep for me, and I can barely contain the hot, hard pleasure that she's mine.

I let my hands travel over her a little longer than absolutely necessary. I'm anchoring her back into me, into touch, checking that she's not straining hard enough to hurt herself. Her muscles ripple happily under my stroking. She hasn't nearly hit her limits with the restraints yet.

Good, because I'm not nearly done playing.

And this time I want to play with her head a little more.

I look up and find her watching me, and I give her the gaze touchstone she needs. Subconsciously or not, she nailed her desires in the photos she chose. Face up, all the way. It's a lot more intense, and most subs instinctively head for the comfort of facedown and the back of their own eyelids.

Not mine. She wants to see her Dom.

She wants to see me.

I reach for the small warmer on the side of the bench and pull out the lube. Time for sensations of a different kind. I squirt out a tiny amount and reach for the nipple closest to me. A test on skin that won't be as sensitive as where I'm headed next.

She smiles and arches a little into my touch. Her eyes start to haze and then snap open as the particular side effects of this lube kick into gear. I can feel it on my fingers too. Warm, insistent tingling.

I give it long enough to make sure she isn't going to have any kind of reaction I don't want and then fill up both my hands with her luscious breasts, working in the lube and enjoying the tingle and the flush it raises in her skin. Her eyes are glued to the motion of my thumbs.

I grin. I won't pull out the mirrors today, but someday I'm going to let this woman see me touching her every damn where.

Her eyes shoot up to mine when I fill my hand with lube and head between her legs. The sound she makes might be words, but it isn't anything close to lightning, so I keep going, spreading spicy and hot into her folds, over her thighs, down into her ass crack, which makes her gasp in ways that tell me that's going to be very interesting territory to play in, too.

I push one of the magic buttons on Milo's bench, lowering part of the bench under her ass and transforming it into a stool that will put me into the kind of cockpit that only a Dom can truly appreciate. I keep sliding my fingers through her folds as I climb in, situating myself between her legs. I run my hands up her thighs and look up, right into her eyes.

I picked this bench for this moment.

Because my sub wants to watch—and when she does, I want her to see me.

Chapter Nineteen

SCORPIO

He's looking at me like he's a dying man and I'm his last meal.

That's all I can think, even though I'm spread wide open for him and he's covered me in some kind of goo that has my parts zinging like they're wired to an amp and I'm trussed up so thoroughly I can barely move.

His hands are touching me again, that gentle stroking that says I'm his and I'm safe and he's got me, no matter what just happened and what's coming next. Magician hands. Hands that know me in ways I can't even believe are possible.

I expected him to fire me up. I never expected him to know how to gentle me back down.

Not like this. Not this big man with the fierce eyes who won't let me look away.

His slides his hands back down to my inner thighs, and I know we're done with the gentle. He runs lube-slicked thumbs up the crack of my ass, and I feel myself tensing. I know I marked this as a soft limit. I hope I can give him that. The edge suddenly feels very sharp.

His eyes are watching mine, and I don't try to hide it. I

don't think I could—I'm spread wide open to him in more ways than one.

His face shifts, and my Dom is back, voice full of gravel and sternness. "Do you need your safeword, beautiful?"

We didn't discuss traffic lights. "Yellow."

His nod is solemn—and his thumbs are still making their circles, over my seat bones and back up my ass crack. Spreading the warm, tingling fire.

I can feel the fight inside me. Wanting to relax. Wanting to snark and push him away and make this so much less about me than it is right now.

His hand reaches for something that looks like a skinny egg with feet. He brings it close to my ass and smears it with lube. I clench as he pushes it against me, seeking entry. My brain is flailing, seeking an exit, running from what he's asking me to do.

And then the egg starts to vibrate, and every nerve in my ass and everywhere else lights on fire.

I hear his warm, dark chuckle. "Like that, do you?"

He's totally got the wrong verb. I'm breaking apart, awash in the sensation of snapping from on the brink of using my safeword to wondering exactly how much I have to beg for him to stick this thing in my ass and leave it there forever.

Clearly he knows it. The egg is demanding entry, pushing in ways that aren't remotely gentle against muscles that aren't remotely ready for this.

His eyes are telling me I can do it anyhow. That he knows I want this, I need this, and he's willing to demand things of me that I would never demand of myself. I stop trying to relax my ass and just sink into his eyes instead, into the soft leather that's holding me and the warm fire all over my skin and the relentless need inside me to be what he's asking me to be.

The egg stops vibrating, but it doesn't stop its slow, inexorable invasion of my ass. The fight inside me comes back to life.

"Take all of it." Harlan's voice snaps into the sudden silence.

I'm trying. Every cell of my body is trying, but it feels as big as a watermelon, even though my eyes totally know that it isn't.

He just keeps pushing. And then there's a pop, and a wild feeling of fullness, and his eyes looking at me with that crazy pride again.

He smiles, and his fingers move into my wet, slick folds. "That was the hard part, beautiful. Now comes the part that's just for me. I'm going to fuck you with my fingers, and I want you to make all the noise you know how to make."

I'm already moaning, writhing into the restraints as two fingers plunge into me and his thumb starts doing things to my clit that should be illegal in all fifty states.

His other hand holds my folds open. "You're wet and swollen and gorgeous." His fingers slide out of me long enough to run up and down the sides of my clit, jacking me up to a totally new level of crazy.

My legs strain against the restraints. He puts a hand on my low belly to hold me down and plunges his fingers into me, hard and fast and insistent.

And then the egg in my ass starts to vibrate again and whatever is left of me shatters all over his hands.

Chapter Twenty

SCORPIO

I don't know when I realize I'm me again.

I'm not in cuffs anymore, not spread open in front of Harlan's ravening eyes. I'm curled into him, drenched in skin and heartbeat and absolute, tender safety.

"Welcome back."

I hear the rumbling from beside my ear, feel his big hands shifting me a little.

"I've got water for you, beautiful. Drink for me."

I do, like a baby bird that has no idea it has wings yet. And when my throat is back to feeling like it belongs to me, I bury back into his chest. Into heartbeat. Into the ridiculous bliss of in-between.

He holds me for what feels like forever.

My stomach lets out a growl loud enough to be heard in California.

Harlan chuckles and kisses the top of my head. "Ready for something to eat?"

I stick my head up and discover we're sprawled in the monster velvet bed—and on the bedside table is a tray full of enough food that there might even be a little left over for the man in bed with me.

A tray of food that wasn't there before. I feel myself stiffening.

He reaches over and pulls the tray closer. "Ari brought it. I hoped you'd be okay with that. You went deep enough that I didn't want to leave."

I open my mouth for the bite he's bringing my way. "Thank you."

His hand strokes my cheek. "If I screwed up, you need to tell me. I heard you loud and clear that you don't want people to see."

She probably only saw me drooling. I manage to swallow before I talk with my mouth full again. "You did good. Ari's not people."

He laughs. "She'll be happy to hear that." He keeps feeding me, like he knows that my arms haven't found their operations manual yet.

I don't tell him even when they do. I'm finally understanding what I've fallen into.

He feeds me, bite by tiny bite, until I groan and turn away. "Done. Full. You can eat the rest."

"I'll tell Ari to bring more next time."

He sounds amused. I push myself back far enough that I can see his face. "You should have seen me after gigs. The guys used to joke that I could consume my body weight in chicken wings."

He's full-on grinning at me now. "I'm duly warned."

I watch as he makes quick work of what's left on the tray. "I might possibly be a greedy sub."

"Mmm." His eyes twinkle at me. "In more ways than one."

I can feel the embarrassment rising in my cheeks.

"Dammit, Emily's supposed to be the one you guys make blush."

His fingers stroke the breast he can reach. "Oh, I've just started making you all pink and rosy and delectable."

That doesn't help the flush go away. "Cut it out. I know how this works. We did the fun stuff and now we have to talk until the kitchen runs out of food and leaves us to crawl begging into the night."

His eyes shift to serious before I can even blink. "Yes, we talk. And my sub doesn't get to use her mouth to push away from whatever she doesn't want me to know."

Shit. I freeze, deer in the headlights. "Crap. Sorry."

He kisses my forehead. "It's okay. It's part of how you're trying to slide back into your skin. I just need you to keep talking to me while you do that. Your poker face didn't make it past the first orgasm, but this works better if I hear words instead of just reading your mind."

All that does is plant my brain squarely back in my first orgasm. "I didn't know I could do that."

His fingers are twiddling with me, so gently I'm not even sure he knows he's doing it. "Do what, beautiful?"

"Come just from you playing with my nipples."

I see it, the streak of pure male pride that has nothing to do with being a Dom and everything to do with being a very self-satisfied caveman. I hide a grin. That guy and I need to get to know each other better.

He shifts us around so we're lying on our sides, facing each other. His hand kneads my ass gently. "What else did you learn?"

I feel the first answer that spurts into my head and the instinctive urge to hide it away, shut it down, cover it with snark. I try not to do any of those things. "The flogger. I've seen some of the scenes here, and that wasn't something I liked watching very much."

His eyes are drinking mine. "Why?"

I grimace. "Pain. I don't like the idea that people get off on it. That I might."

"Did you?"

No clues. No body language. No idea what he wants to hear. "It didn't hurt, exactly. It felt like hot rain, and then it got less pinprick and more like this spreading deal."

He's nodding. Listening. "Did you want more?"

I remember the bereft loneliness when he stopped. "I didn't want it to end."

He strokes my cheek so fucking softly it makes me want to cry. "Did you want it deeper? Harder? Into pain?"

He's asked gently enough that I can actually listen for my own answer. "No."

Only then does he let out the breath I didn't know he's been holding. "Good. No judgment from me if that's what you need, but I don't like going there."

I can see that. He's letting me see that. "Den mother."

His grin is lopsided. "Yeah. There are lots of edges to ride. Pain's not mine."

But he still took me close enough that I could figure out if it was mine. I close my eyes, suddenly realizing exactly how generous he is.

His hand is back on my cheek. "What?"

"You have a very big heart, tough guy."

He scowls.

I scowl right back. "You asked. If you don't want my truth, then don't ask for it."

He takes a breath that mostly comes out as a growl. "Yeah. Sorry." He runs an apologetic hand down my side. "So baby floggers and sensation play are fun for you, but we're not angling for pain. Yellow's a good word if you need to let me know to back off or slow down a little. We didn't talk about that before, but you used it just right today."

I know what I used it on. "Sorry—I know I got kind of wimpy with that egg thing."

He grins. "Anal plug. No calling my toys any cutesy names."

This time the snark is rising up from the right place. "If they're headed inside me, I'll call them whatever I want to call them."

He gives my ass an amused swat. "Then you'll pay for it."

I reach forward and kiss his cheek, because this tender crap is killing me and I want more of it. "Deal."

Chapter Twenty-One

HARLAN

In fifteen years, I've done about every flavor of aftercare there is. This is the really good kind. The kind where a sub can rise up out of where she's been and meet me on totally level ground and dig into the energy of having just done something fucking amazing together.

Scorpio's totally sliding back into her skin, but she's letting me touch it. Staying open. Telling me truth.

I just want to cuddle into her and stay there for about a week. Right after I fuck her silly so that my cock doesn't die of delayed gratification. Or even without that.

Which is a thought I've had in the last fifteen years exactly never.

I stroke her delectable ass again and my hand isn't totally steady. Fuck. I need to get my head back into my job, because this debrief isn't nearly over. "The anal play pushed on you." Harder than I'd expected for a woman who's done the kind of time she has on Fettered's couches. No way this is shame for her.

She's nodding, and I can see the confusion in her eyes. "Yeah. I'm not sure why."

I let my fingers travel a little closer to the region we're talking about. My hand is steadier now—it knows how to do this part. "How does it feel when I head in that direction now?"

She's already shifting, spreading for me—and tensing up. Which tells me plenty, but I want to hear it from her. I take her leg, pull her thigh up over my hip, and keep stroking her ass crack. She'll learn far more from her body on this than she will from her mind.

She's quiet for a long time, following my hands from inside her skin. When her eyes finally unhaze, she looks a little sheepish. "I don't think anal play is the problem. I think it's a control thing. I didn't have any, but I had time to think. With the flogger, I got overwhelmed with sensation so fast there wasn't time for my head to get in the way."

Smart, intuitive sub. "How close were you to your safeword before I used the vibrator button?"

Her eyes get really serious. "Very. Sorry."

I have her chin in my hand so fast neither of us knows what's landed. "Don't ever apologize for that. *Ever.* You need your safeword, you even think you need it, *you use it.* You went to lots of edges for me today, and you'll go to lots more, and you never need to feel weak or sorry or like you failed me in any way if we find one you don't want to touch. Got it?"

She's staring at me, eyes huge. And then this totally soft, fragile smile sneaks onto her face. "Yeah."

Every Dom instinct I have jumps to attention. The ones that heard her words about surrender that isn't weak. The ones that saw her lean into a flogger and draw her lines on pain with easy bravery, and then nearly safeword on a kind of play that's all about vulnerability. The ones that have heard her apologize more in this bed in an hour than she should in a year.

She's just handed me the keys to something huge, even if she doesn't know it yet.

Her sharpest edge isn't pain or owning her needs or surrendering control.

It's fear of being weak.

I cuddle her in closer to me, because I know the stark intimacy of this moment, even if she won't for a while. I know there's no rush. She's mine now, and I'm not letting her go. Not until we unlock the cage she's just let me glimpse.

I stroke her from shoulder to hip, loving the curves of her. "We can stay here as long as you want. More food? Nap? Wild, crazy sex?"

She grins at me. "Why do I think you're not serious about that last one?"

I swat her ass again, just because I can. "Topping from the bottom already?"

She sticks out her tongue. "Am not. You brought it up."

I did and she's right and while we'd clearly both be pretty damn happy if I took her up on the easy invitation she's exuding, I know better. We need to have the lines clear and straight and true between us before we blur them like that, or we aren't going to get to the edges she needs.

The ones I can smell.

She traces a finger over my tats, as if she's reading the writing on my wall as easily as I read hers. "I'm actually coming back here tonight."

That wasn't what I expected to hear. I pull up the club schedule in my mental calendar, wondering what the heck she's coming back for—and roll my eyes when I find the answer. "Charades night?"

She grins. "Yup. Ari invited me ages ago."

That's interesting. Charades might sound mellow, but it's generally not an event where non-members get invited, even really easygoing, accepting ones. I might have the best nose in the business, but Ari's not far behind. I'm not the only one who smelled this sub on her way.

I tug Scorpio into my chest. If I'm suddenly attending charades night, I need some sleep first. "Nap. Food. Then you can go home and put on something sexy to wear while you sit in my lap tonight."

I can feel her eyebrows winging up. "I'm not playing charades from your lap."

I laugh, and I can feel it vibrating both of us. "Want to bet on that?"

She doesn't answer. I grin. Smart sub.

Chapter Twenty-Two

SCORPIO

"Settle down, people."

I haven't moved since Ari plunked me down on a stool at the bar beside Marla and told me to stay there, but her clarion command has the rest of the crowd finding a perch and mostly getting quiet. I know about half the people in the lounge, and the other half seem to know me. But I'm acutely aware I'm the newbie in the room. Nobody's said a thing—but it's obvious in the way they touch each other, know each other, crack up laughing with nothing more than a wink or a growl.

I see Harlan sliding in from the dungeon and let out a breath I hadn't known I was holding. He leans against the door and looks me up and down, and that fast, my skin remembers what it is to be touched by him.

Marla chuckles quietly beside me. "Ooh, you picked a good one for your first ride."

I've sat in this lounge and heard that kind of teasing for years now—but this is the first time it's personal. "I think he mostly chose me."

That gets another laugh, and then we're all turning our focus to the woman running the show. Ari's dressed in a red silk teddy, tight black latex leggings, and enough personal charm to run the known world without even having to work hard.

She winks at me, and I feel pretty damn happy to be part of that world.

"Okay, people. Basic charades rules, and if you don't know what those are, someone will be happy to spank you if you goof up. It's musical tonight—song titles and lyrics, and some of you are probably old enough that you're going to hate me by the end of the night. No serious scening while we play, and the winning team gets to name the song the losing team has to dance to."

Some ham in the corner of the couch furthest from me stands up and starts shaking his hips, sending a bunch of silver discs shimmying merrily.

Ari laughs. "Sit down, Ronny—you haven't lost yet."

"Yes, Mistress." He sits down, blowing her kisses.

I get the message. This isn't a night where subs are going to be on their good behavior. I glance over at Harlan, grinning— and find him devouring me with his eyes.

Damn.

Ari holds up a hand. "Before we start, five-minute break for those of you who need to pee, adjust your anal plugs, or have a chat with your Dom or sub. Limits matter tonight just like any other night, so if you don't know what yours are, sort them out fast."

I'm trying to imagine what limits might be necessary for a miming game, but most of the obviously paired people in the room are leaning their heads together, so clearly Ari understands something I don't. I'm beginning to suspect that there's a whole lot of somethings I'm clueless on right now.

An arm slides around my waist from the back, and I'm snugged up against hard Dom muscle faster than I can bleat in protest. I struggle momentarily, not at all sure I'm ready for this kind of public claiming.

The growl in my ear isn't remotely sympathetic.

I freeze, registering Harlan's body language—and how many eyes are subtly and not so subtly turned our way. Oops. I relax into him, apologizing in the best way I know how.

His arm eases. "I should have warned you that I can be an overbearing bastard."

I grin—at the moment he's nuzzling into my shoulder and doing a good impression of a teddy bear. "So tell me why Ari thinks we need to be talking right now. The rules seem pretty clear."

"Those are the club rules that apply to everyone. She wants to make sure you know my rules for you tonight."

That has my body wanting to tense up again, but I do my best to relax. "I just came here to play charades."

Another growl. "You came here as my sub."

I freaking wish his gravel didn't make me quiver so damn fast.

His free hand cups my breast, brushes over my nipple. "Shh. Easy, beautiful. You can set ground rules if you need to as well."

I'm so lost. "This is charades."

He picks me up and turns me around, and I suddenly find myself standing between his legs as he leans on the stool I just vacated. His eyes are full of amusement. "I could tell you that you need to sit naked in my lap all night, or I could insert your favorite vibrating egg and tell you that you can't come unless your team wins."

"Are you freaking kidding me?"

His laugh rumbles out into the room. His hands are solid on my hips, his thumbs rubbing circles on my belly that are anything but soothing. "Just letting you know some of what you might see tonight."

I gulp. I'm so not in Kansas anymore. "So what are your rules for me?"

He grins. "Just one. Sometime before you go home tonight, I want you to ask nicely to come for me. It can be as private or as public as you want."

It's all I can do not to rub my legs together.

He's watching me in the way that I already know means he's seeing everything, and his eyes are gleaming. "Or maybe I'll just slide my fingers into your pussy right now and let everyone hear how beautiful you are when you shatter."

The whimper that escapes is me is wanton and pissy and more than a little desperate.

He brushes his thumbs over my nipples. "One orgasm tonight, and only one. You decide when, you decide where."

I can barely breathe. "I guess that leaves you deciding how hard, how fast, and how long, huh?"

His eyes go molten. "And how many times I'll be spanking your ass before you get to come." His hands on my nipples pull me in, and he's not being gentle anymore. "I'll be keeping track, beautiful. Every sass, every swing of those hips where you try to tease your Dom, every time you think something sexy and don't come over and tell me what's got you all hot and bothered."

I'm so fucking wet I can feel it starting to soak into my jeans.

He smiles, and I know he can tell. "We'll start with three for the sexy outfit you didn't wear tonight."

I'm in jeans and a tank top. "This is as sexy as punk rockers get."

Whatever he's going to say is interrupted by clapping from behind me.

"Time's up." Ari sounds way too damn cheerful. "Find your team couch and keep your hands wherever they're supposed to be."

I turn around, trying to pull my brain out of wherever Harlan has just sent it, and discover that lots of the people in the lounge are now in various shades of halfway naked, and more than one sub has a rosy ass or nipple clamps or the slightly stilted walk that means they're wearing things I can't see.

I breathe in, knowing I've landed in the big leagues, and feel Harlan's hand at my back. Steadying me. Pushing me forward. Reminding me I have every right to be here, and that I know most of these people and like them a lot.

Ari grins and waves me over to her couch. She shimmies over to one side to make room for me and then gasps, glaring at a hot young guy in leathers on a different couch.

Marla laughs from my other side. "He's just waiting for a chance to paddle you, Ari—don't get his hopes up so fast."

Ari snickers and then sucks in her breath again. This time she moans a little before she finally exhales. "Damn. He's got evil timing." She takes a couple more breaths and then shoots me a look. "You okay with this, sweetie?"

I can see Marla tuning in too. Two women who know the deep end really well, making sure the newbie doesn't go under. Something inside me unfurls into their solid warmth. I've sat with friends riding highs, riding crashes, doing deep damage to their ability to live happy and sane in the world. This is so much different. So much better.

I grin at Ari. "Harlan says I only get one orgasm tonight. Bet you come before I do."

Her eyes flash with hilarity and pride and competitive fire. "You're on, chickadee." She looks over at Harlan, sitting quietly on a couch between Damon and a guy I don't know.

"Get her riled, will you? I need her to come before I do. Cookies are on the line."

I splutter, but I know better than to fight sneaky tactics with petty whining. I look at the man she was glaring at earlier. "I'm pretty easy, so you might want to get on that. I hear she likes to bake naked."

He grins at me, and suddenly Ari's squirming again.

And oddly, as I sit between one woman on the brink of orgasm and another one who's laughing so hard she might pee at any moment—I feel as easy and as loved and as accepted as I've ever been.

Chapter Twenty-Three

HARLAN

I need her in my lap. Not to stake my claim, but just because I have the crazy need to touch her and hold her and feel her against my skin, and to honor the journey she's walking tonight.

But I've already figured out that she needs to walk this part alone. To sit in the middle of my tribe and feel her way to however she wants to belong. Marla and Ari are making sure she has every possible opportunity—and where they go, everyone else will follow.

I wonder if my sub has any idea just how well everyone in this room is reading her. Her poker face blew wide open on a rock wall late last night and it's never come back. Her bravery and loneliness and hope and longing are written all over her.

Along with how desperately she wants to ride my fingers again.

Letting her pick when and where isn't a beginner game. It's going to confuse the lines and I'm going to have to fix that later, and I know better than to rile up a newbie sub this much without giving her anything obvious to hold on to. But she asked for the times in between, and this is one way to get them, even if the rules aren't as clear and easy.

I watch Scorpio's face light up with laughter and more than a little embarrassment as Ari's Dom for the night has her squeaking and stuffing a hand between her legs.

Damon and I are keeping an eye on him, because this is his first night here, but so far he totally has Ari's number. It's good to see. Not very many people can get that far with her—not with her still this happy and obviously angling for whatever they put on the punishment menu together.

I grin at my sub. I'm pretty damn pleased with that particular item on our menu tonight too. It was a last-minute addition, a way to have fun with her and give her permission to let her mouth run free. I see her looking at me and I hold up another finger. I don't even know what she's done to deserve it, and it doesn't matter. Her bent over my knee, ass squirming in the air, is a reward I plan to collect on.

Scorpio sees my finger, sighs, and shakes her head ruefully. Then she holds up three fingers, which nearly blasts a cock-sized hole in my vaunted self-control.

She's getting to me, this sub who likes to let loose and who likes to play and who isn't remotely afraid of her edges or mine or the stuff that is somehow leaking out into the middle. I get up and walk over behind her couch and slide my head down beside her ear. "For someone who's never been spanked before, you seem pretty sure you're going to like it."

She's shivering, but manages a cocky grin. "Who says I haven't been spanked?"

Ari snickers beside me. I raise an eyebrow at her Dom. "I hear she likes to bake naked."

He grins and obliges me, and I nuzzle into my sub as Ari turns into a puddle of girl trying to withhold orgasm and rapidly losing. "I say."

Scorpio's having a hard time ignoring the action right beside her. Her eyes are on me, but her breathing is going haywire.

My respect for Ari's new Dom ratchets up sharply when he turns off the remote about half a second before she loses it entirely. I hold up two more fingers for my sub and walk away, leaving her to figure out why.

It would be fun to have her in my lap for the rest of the night, but it's more fun watching her reactions—and for that I need to see her face. I join Emily's team and send Quint packing. He's got the best view of the face I need to see. He goes without a murmur of protest and takes his tiny fireball of a trainee sub with him. She's clearly not new to the lifestyle or he wouldn't have her here. She casts a knowing glance at me as she leaves, and I know it's not only the Doms watching the action tonight.

I grin. I like it when people watch.

Chapter Twenty-Four

SCORPIO

Ari lurches to her feet long enough to grab a velvet bag and toss it to one of the other couches. "You guys are up first." Her voice is breathy, like she's still fighting off massive distraction.

I'm not sure whether to be sorry my Dom left or sorry he didn't stay.

After some jostling, the tiny sub on Quint's lap stands up. She looks down at the strip of paper in her hand, grins at her team, and holds up three fingers.

"Three words." Her people have clearly done this before.

She flashes three fingers again.

"Third word."

She motions Quint to stand up with a come-hither look that has half the guys in the room volunteering.

He raises an eyebrow. "Spanking bench."

Ari hoots beside me. "That's two words, Quint—learn to count." She makes it almost through her sentence before she starts squirming again.

I'm damn glad Harlan doesn't have a remote in his hand. His eyes are trouble enough. And his cute little rule that means I'm going to be thinking about his fingers in my pussy all damn night. Or my first spanking.

I glance his way and see him holding up two fingers.

Fuck. I hope Ari's squirming enough to cover the fact that I'm not sitting very still either.

The tiny sub sticks her hands in Quint's lap, first close together, and then moving one out. Measuring an invisible inflating penis.

Emily, sitting primly on the end of the couch, grins. "Elongation."

Damon laughs so hard from his team couch that he nearly chokes. "Really, sweetheart? Name one song with that in the lyrics."

The tiny sub swats Damon and motions Emily to repeat her word, and then makes shrinking motions with her hands. *Make the word shorter.* Emily grins again. "Long. 'All Night Long'."

Her whole team piles off the couch for a victory dance, and Quint tosses Emily into the air. "We are so winning this thing." He looks over at Damon. "I'm keeping her. She's way too smart for you."

Emily rolls her eyes and pokes Quint in the ribs. "If you get me spanked again today, I will get even."

Quint lets go of her like she's electrocuted him, which has Damon laughing again.

They manage to get themselves under control and back on their couch in some semblance of a well-behaved team, and then it's our turn. After some elbowing and giggling, Marla pushes herself up and plucks a strip of paper from Ari's bag. She grins and holds up three fingers and flashes them twice.

I've got this. Wedding planners for the win. "Three words, third word."

She walks over and kisses the man she came with. He pulls

her in for a far more thorough kiss, and he doesn't stick with just her lips.

Ari snorts beside me. "Hot."

Marla jumps off Jacob, which gets her a swat that mostly misses and a growl that promises this will come back to bite her later. She ignores him and dances over to Doxy and points at her shiny engagement ring, holding one finger in the air.

I say the obvious. "First word. Circle. Ring."

The guy on the end of our couch looks confused. "'Circle of Hot'?"

I shake my head. We are so losing this thing. "Do none of you listen to music ever? 'Ring of Fire'."

Ari pouts beside me. "Dammit, Scorpio—we wanted to see Marla's clit ring."

I don't even know what that is—and I suddenly realize that the point of this night doesn't have a whole lot to do with being a good charades player. I suddenly feel like a newbie, and not in a good way.

Marla walks over to Jacob and eases herself into his lap, gasping a little as she sits. Then she winks at me and pulls me right off my ledge of stupid. These people aren't trying to sideline me—my own ignorance is doing that, but the only one who cares about that is me.

I thought I knew this world, but in this moment, the difference between being a tourist and a resident is excruciatingly clear.

Chapter Twenty-Five

HARLAN

This night is way too fucking long.

My team is so far ahead nobody's going to catch up, which is totally Damon's fault. He hasn't figured out how to distract his sub, and Emily's singlehandedly keeping us at the top of the leaderboard. Which is quite the trick when you're a pretty woman in a demure green dress sitting on a team couch full of Doms who've clearly failed every acting class they ever attended.

I shake my head as Scorpio's team takes possession of the velvet bag and Ari gets up again. She looks at her strip of paper, and then something odd crosses her face and she walks over and whispers into the ear of her Dom.

He gives her a look I can't read and nods. Permission granted, for whatever it is.

She ditches her high-heel boots and latex leggings and lets down her hair, and suddenly she's Ari in floaty red lingerie, looking young and ethereal and dreamy.

I have no idea what word she's going after. It doesn't matter. My eyes are on my sub. She hasn't moved, hasn't done anything obvious to grab my attention. But she's watching Ari, and only Ari, and Scorpio's eyes are yearning and running scared again—and the spell doesn't break until the one Dom in the room who clearly didn't fail his acting classes bends Ari back in one of those swoony kisses that looks like it belongs on the cover of a romance novel.

Then Ari snaps back into being Ari, her Dom pushes whatever evil button he has in his pocket, and she comes in his arms, hard enough to cause an earthquake and cursing a blue streak, and Scorpio's laughing along with everyone else as the boldest sub in the house loses her bet and plants a huge kiss on the cheek of the man who made it happen.

I'm still stuck in the moment where my sub's eyes went all soft and haunted. It's the second time in two days I've seen it. Fear and longing.

Fuck. I just want to hold her tonight. I don't want to push her.

But that's the man talking.

The Dom can see her need.

There's an edge coming, and we need to face it, and I'm going to need to help her. But she asked more of me, and somehow I need to give her that too. The fun and the safety and the deep goodness of the in-between. To spank her and tease her and make her come and then tuck her in next to me and hold her while she sleeps.

Even if that makes tomorrow harder for both of us.

Chapter Twenty-Six

SCORPIO

One minute I'm sitting on the couch laughing, listening to Ari curse and mutter, Marla still shaking with merriment beside me. The next I'm slung over the shoulder of an impatient caveman and watching all my new friends laugh upside down as he storms out of the room.

I'm damn tempted to swat his ass and make him put me down. "The fuck?"

"That can be arranged too." He sounds far too pleased by that thought.

I sway for a moment when he puts me down. We're in the dungeon, and that's about all I have time to register before he sits down on a spanking bench, grins at me, and holds up two fingers. "Two more for the smart-ass thoughts you had as I dragged you in here."

He's definitely gone all Dom on me—but there's a lightness to it. A teasing. And damn if it doesn't make me want whatever's coming next. I glance over at the door and the big ears I'm sure are on the other side.

"Eyes on me, beautiful."

My head snaps back to him before I can even think.

"There are consequences to yanking on your Dom's chain." He pats his leg. "Drop your jeans and bend over my lap, ass in the air."

A whimper sneaks out, and I slap a hand over my mouth at the raw desire in that sound and what it must tell him.

He reaches up and pulls down my wrist. "Never try to hide what you feel. Not from me." The corners of his lips turn up. "Looking forward to this, are you?"

I suck in a breath, not sure whether to shake my head or nod. "Maybe. I think so. I don't know."

He chuckles, and then his eyes do that stern thing again. "Pants down. Ass up."

I thought this might feel like being a kid in the principal's office. I'm so wrong. Not with the way his eyes are devouring me. I somehow manage to get my belt undone, and my baggy jeans fall down without any help from me.

He slides a hand between my legs and growls. "Not once tonight did you come over and whisper in my ear and tell me what was turning you on. Tell me now and maybe this spanking gets shorter."

I'm not sure that's actually incentive, but his hand in my pussy definitely is. "I loved watching Ari's Dom tease her. I know this is called play, but with them, it actually looked fun. Silly." I hitch a breath at what his fingers are doing. "And Quint kept touching his sub, even when he looked like his attention was totally somewhere else."

I close my eyes, and his fingers stop. Damn. "I think I'd like to be in your lap sometime. At an event like this." I scrunch my face, because this last part is going to be the hardest, and look at him because I need to see his eyes. "And I know they're listening out there, at least some of them, and it's making me wet and bothered."

His fingers slide up inside me. "And?"

Damn him and his all-seeing eyes. "I'm proud to be here as yours tonight."

He growls, and suddenly I'm over his lap and my face is pasted into the spanking bench and my feet are flailing. "Then let them hear you be proud, beautiful." His hand rubs my ass, squeezing. I grab the side of the bench with one hand and his pant leg with the other.

I'm so ready for this.

Chapter Twenty-Seven

HARLAN

I'm about to fucking punish a woman who has just slayed me with her words. I shake my head, damn glad she was getting every bit of the fun side of this spanking before she changed it into something else. She's earned every swat, with her mouth and her attitude and her unwavering openness to what I've been asking of her and to what she wants to give.

The people on the other side of that door already fucking love her, but this is going to cement her place in this community. In the hearts of the people who are my family.

She jerks when I land my hand on her ass, but there's no withdrawal. No shock. I grin. Not all edges are hard and sharp. This one is soft and curvy and I have a lapful of woman who can't wait for me to spank her some more.

There are times when being a really cooperative Dom is its own reward. I swat her again, setting up an alternating rhythm that her punk-rock heart can sing with. And when she starts to push her ass up, asking for more, I give it to her.

I keep it light. This isn't remotely about pain. It's about membership, and she's done all she needs to do to earn hers.

She's wiggling like sin, trying to get my hand to land on her pussy. I pin her down tighter with my free hand and then move the spanking closer to where she wants it. She starts moaning, thrashing in my lap. I don't remind her of the very quiet audience on the other side of the dungeon door. Every person in the lounge will respect the hell out of what she's doing here, and she's far enough gone that the only thing she's hearing is my hand.

That's as deep as I want to take her tonight. We still need to walk back through that door.

I move my hand a little lower, deliver a couple of much softer swats to her dripping arousal. Her eyes snap open and somehow they find mine. "Harlan. Please."

She's asking for the orgasm I've promised her, but it's so damn much fun to mess with her. I land my hand on her pussy again, loving the spurting wetness. "More of this?"

It blows my Dom ego up like a balloon when she pauses, clearly considering it. "Later. I need to come." The last word comes out mostly as a whimper.

She's so fucking beautiful. I slick my palm with her wetness and then rub in hot, tight circles over her swollen folds. I'm not aiming for finesse—this isn't going to take long.

She comes, shrieking against my hand and my knee and the spanking bench that has just become her world, and I can hear the moans and murmurs on the other side of the door as more than one sub clearly joins her.

I grin and collect up the hot sweaty mess of woman in my lap and go find us a comfortable chair. Part of this scene is going to be walking back into the lounge, but first I need to hold her. I want to breathe in the awesome, playful, brave sassiness of her and just appreciate the moment. I laugh as I sit down, trying to contend with the fact that she's still got her jeans around her ankles and her boots on. Newbie Dom error, but I'll deal. I tuck her into my lap and make sure I can reach the water nearby. She drank an ocean of it the last time we scened together.

It doesn't take her long to come around this time—she went down fast and she's coming up that way too.

When I see the focus slide back into her eyes, I hand her the water bottle and pick her up, blanket, boots, jeans around her ankles, and all. Her eyes fly up to mine. "Where are we going?"

I grin down at her sexy, mussed-up face. "To see if anyone's still playing charades."

She has time to raise one skeptical eyebrow and then Quint's sweeping the door open for me and I'm carrying her into the middle of the couches that have been re-arranged into a neat semi-circle facing the dungeon. Just in case Scorpio needs any more clues.

She takes in the shifted furniture and the number of subs sitting in Dom laps looking happy and flustered, and makes a strangled sound in my arms.

Ari laughs from her guy's knees, his hand still between her legs. "Thanks, Scorpio. You have some seriously contagious orgasms." She tosses me a bottle of the club's oil, which is magic for parts that have been well used. "Sounds like her ass could use some of this, and maybe a few other places too."

The tiny sub in Quint's arms is still glassy-eyed, but he winks at the woman in my lap. "Next time see if you can hold off a little longer, sweetheart. You made some of us have to work pretty fast to catch up."

All Scorpio can manage is a squawk.

I squeeze her ass, since it's handy, and sit down on a couch with Damon and Emily. Scorpio looks over at her boss, sitting primly beside Fettered's owner with bright-red cheeks and one of her nipples showing, and ducks her head into my chest. I hold her for a minute, surprised she's this embarrassed—and then I realize she's laughing.

I shake my head and turn her around so she can't pull that shit—and so that she can see all the smiles. All the appreciation and respect and welcome and love.

She tilts her head back on my shoulder and drinks it all in.

I hold the bottle of magic oil and wonder whether I need to dump some on my heart.

Chapter Twenty-Eight

HARLAN

It's getting too damn cold to be walking around late at night. I keep Scorpio's hand in mine and watch her for shivering. Hell, I watch her for everything.

She stuffs her other hand in her pocket and grins at me. "Stop fretting. I grew up in Minnesota. This is practically like summer."

I realize just how much I know about her—and how little. "How'd you end up here?"

"School. Band. Boy."

I don't know if that's multiple choice or just the short version of a long story, but it's clearly not what she wants to talk about right now. I look over at her again, making sure she's as solid as she sounds.

She rolls her eyes at me. "Tonight was awesome and you can stop worrying about me."

I can't, but I can at least try to pretend. "That was a pretty big scene, even if it doesn't feel like it. Public stuff can bring up a lot of issues."

She shrugs and squeezes my hand. "You warned me we'd be

playing that way. A collection of my friends and old-hand club members is a pretty friendly public."

I stop and turn her toward me, because I need to see her eyes. "Even when they got off on your very noisy pleasure?"

She's looking embarrassed now, but she meets my gaze. "People used to get off on my singing too. Not quite like that, but close enough. I like sharing. I like knowing other people caught a piece of the good thing I was riding tonight."

She's so damn beautiful. "Your boss was looking pretty happy."

The sound that comes out of my gorgeous sub is almost a giggle. "So was yours."

"Damon's found something different since Emily showed up." Something that maybe the rest of us are suddenly looking for, and that's shaking me. I thought I had the life I wanted. "He daydreams in his office when he thinks we aren't watching."

Scorpio's grin is big enough to light up half the night. "Emily put her ribbon samples in the fridge yesterday. And one morning last week her shoes didn't match."

I look down at her hand in mine. I'm beginning to have an idea of just how brains get scrambled like that.

Scorpio cuddles into my side as we start walking again. "Who's Ari's new guy?"

"He's visiting from a club in L.A. He's basically her counterpart down there. He came up here to learn from the best." And apparently she decided to play with him. "He was doing a really good job with her, and that's not all that easy."

Scorpio's forehead wrinkles. "Ari's got mad skills."

"Yeah. She can be a good sub for almost anyone, but most guys run into trouble trying to be a Dom for her. They work too hard or they get insecure or they decide they need to prove something or they treat her like a damn trophy."

My wise sub snorts. "I bet she doesn't let them get away with that shit."

Too much sometimes, because she has a soft heart and she wants them to learn. "She's a good trainer, but that can ruin her fun."

I feel the sudden tensing under my arm as we turn into the small apartment building where she lives. "Is it ruining yours? Teaching me how to do this?"

Shit—I walked right into that one. "No." I stop and turn her to face me again. "Tonight was the most fun I've had at the club in a really long time, beautiful." Or out of it.

Her eyes are solemn in the dim of the night. "I want to be what you need."

"Start with being what you need, okay? That's the first step here." That's the Dom answer, and it somehow hurts to say it out loud. Because the man has a different one. The man could be totally happy with what he has right now. The man doesn't want to push.

The Dom wants a chance to see what lives out the other side. Wants to give her that chance. Which is tossing the man in way over his head.

I reach for her, because it's the Dom who's made her promises. "Come sit with me for a minute. I've got something to ask you."

Chapter Twenty-Nine

SCORPIO

He tugs me over to a planter box and pulls me into his lap. My landlady will have fits—I'm pretty sure he's sitting on her prize petunias. I don't say anything, because his energy has totally shifted, and he's making me nervous.

He reaches into his pocket, pulls out a folded-up envelope, and hands it to me. "Which one is it?"

I slowly flip through what he's handed me. It's three of the pictures from Ari's collection. The restraints one I've already given him, and two more. I recognize them both. I look up at him, knowing I'm starting to shake and hating it. "I don't understand." All I know is that he's ruining my high, my really good night, my calm.

Shoving me back on a sharp edge, and I don't want to be there.

His hand is stroking my back before I finish cursing him in my head. Soothing. Demanding. "Which is the one that makes you want something you haven't told me about?"

I'm turning clammy and I'm not even sure why. "I gave you the one I liked the best."

A low, hard growl. "Don't fuck with me, Scorpio."

I look at the other two pictures, frustrated and pissy and ready to kick him in the knees because I'm not hiding anything and he's making me feel like a liar and all they are is two fucking pictures—and then I know. I know exactly what he's seen, and there's no freaking way I can say it out loud.

I glare a hole at the image that's trying to make me weak. "Hard limit."

He stands me up, facing him, and his eyes are full of cold, dark compassion. "That's not what limits are for, beautiful. You don't get to use them to push away something you want. Not when I can see it all over your face."

I want to throw every word of his fucking contract in his face. "This *isn't* what I want." I'm shaking with something hot and mean. "Why are you pushing on me? Tonight was amazing and now I feel like you're throwing dirt on it and telling me I wasn't good enough."

Fire, to fight what I'm really afraid of.

He cups my face in his big, fierce, gentle hands. "You took your place in my world tonight and you were absolutely gorgeous and nobody can take that away from you." He takes a ragged breath, and for the first time in this whole deal, I smell his doubt. "That's not what I'm trying to do here, I promise you."

It's the doubt that does me in. I want so much to cuddle into his chest, but I can't make myself move. "I don't need all the edges. I lived that life once. I won't do it again. I'm fine with just a few of them."

Not this one. Please, not this one.

I can hear his breath, moving in and out. Steadying. His confidence reforming, the gut-deep sense that what he's doing is right. When he finally reaches a hand to my face, his words are gentle, but absolutely solid. "Take the photos with you. Think about them. If this is still a hard limit for you in the morning and you tell me you're doing it for the right reasons, I'll respect that."

He gives me one of those looks that says he sees right into the chambers of my heart. Then he turns and walks away, and not once, down the entire block that I watch him, does he turn and look back.

Damn him to all fourteen levels of hell and back.

I pour myself a bowl of granola, the good kind with chocolate and coconut and little bits of pineapple that I used to eat by the pound to keep sane on the road. It's my ultimate comfort food, but I'm pretty sure granola isn't going to do a darn thing for the storm Harlan has set off inside me.

I stare at the photo that's been propped on my kitchen table for the last hour. I've considered burning it, but that would probably just get me a visit from some nice firefighters who don't want to hear why I'm using a photograph of a chick in a sexy negligée as tinder.

I trace her face with my finger. I know why she sets me off. It's the look in her eyes. The thing I don't want to want. I can tell Harlan—but I know what will happen if I do, and I'm not sure I can stand it.

There are some pieces of me I'm not looking to break.

The knock on my fire-escape door has me jerking so hard I almost dump my granola. I grumble and yank the door open, and blink in surprise when it's Ari on the other side.

She holds up a bakery bag. "Chocolate éclairs. Don't shoot."

I scowl. "Did Harlan send you?"

Her eyebrows fly up. "No. Did he need to?" She walks in and takes the other seat at my table. She's watching me the whole time, just like he does.

"Fuck." I push my granola out of the way and lay my head down on my arms. "You all have the same eyes, and I'm sick and tired of people studying me like I might crack at any moment."

"Oh, boy." A container of orange juice clunks down by my head. "Drink. Now."

I shoot her an evil look. "What, do you all get lessons in the gravel voice thing?"

She taps my nose with her finger and grins. "I give those lessons, girlfriend." She opens the orange juice for me. "I don't know if you're crashing or just cranky, but this should help either way. Bottoms up."

I drink, partly because my insides are suddenly screaming for sweet and tangy, and partly because I can see the warm compassion in her eyes that disappeared from Harlan's last night.

She waits until I finish every drop. Then she opens the bakery bag and pulls out an éclair as big as my head and sets it on the table in front of me.

I manage a smirk. "What, you don't believe in plates?"

She rolls her eyes and pulls out a second éclair. "Sometimes reactions to a scene can kick in hours or days later, and the crash can be physical as well as emotional. Eat."

I snort. "I hope your new boy toy kept you up late last night."

She laughs and takes a huge bite of her éclair. "He did, and I'm starving. I'm also not here to gossip about my night or my Dom's excellent talents with anal play. Talk, girlfriend."

I kick her under the table. "Tease."

She just looks at me.

Bloody hell. "There's a thing. From one of your porn pictures. Something I'm reacting to but I don't want. Harlan's seeing my reaction and he's pushing on me."

"Ah." Her eyes flick to the image that somehow ended up on the floor. "That one?"

So much for anything resembling a private life. "I told him it was a hard limit. He told me I was using that the wrong way."

Ari picks the image up off the floor and looks at it for a long moment. "With most Doms I'd tell you to stick to your guns. You don't need a reason for a hard limit. They're sacred for a reason, just like safewords."

I didn't miss the first part of what she said. "But not with Harlan."

She shrugs, and her eyes are full of steely empathy that makes me flail helplessly. "He's one of the best men I know, and he gets people, way down deep where they sometimes hide the things they most want."

I shudder, because that's the most attractive thing about him—and the most dangerous.

She hands me the photo. "Consider whether maybe your Dom sees something important and he wants to give you a chance to meet it."

Her words are a fist to my gut. "I don't want this."

She reaches for my hands—and she never looks away from my eyes. "I'm going to stick my nose in way deep where it doesn't belong, and Harlan's probably going to kick my ass for it."

I manage a wobbly grin. "I'd like to see him try."

She laughs, and then she leans her forehead into mine. "If this really is a hard line for you, he'll be the first one to respect it, and if he doesn't, there will be people lined up for a mile to beat him up."

"I'm not going to like the rest of this sentence, am I?"

I feel her smile. "You're a smart cookie." She pauses, assembling her words carefully. "There are a lot of Doms who will let you get away with conditional surrender—heck, lots of them won't even notice you're doing it."

I tip my head, remembering what Harlan said about her last night. "That happens to you a lot, doesn't it? That's why you were having so much fun last night. The guy from L.A. is a good catcher."

Her eyebrows shoot up in surprise. "Yeah. He is." She pauses and bites her lower lip. "It's a really big gift when someone can do that." She taps the photo without looking away from me. "I think maybe Harlan's asking for the chance to do that for you."

I close my eyes. I don't know if I can say yes.

Chapter Thirty-One

HARLAN

Damon pushes away his laptop as I walk into his office. "Whoa, what crawled up your ass?"

I want to scowl at him, but my face is already there. "Nothing."

He snorts. "Scorpio did great last night. What happened between then and now?"

I fling myself into the most disreputable chair in his office. "What makes you think I'm having sub problems?"

"You're here early, you're wearing your meanest leathers, and you're sulking in my office." He looks amused. "Do I need any more reasons, or are you going to stop the middle-school crap and tell me what the hell's going on?"

The guy's known me since forever. That's not always an upside. "I don't know yet."

He raises an eyebrow. "Does it have anything to do with Ari texting me that she's going to be late because she dropped by Scorpio's place for breakfast?"

Fuck. "Does she have to stick her nose in every damn thing?"

"Yes. It's what we pay her to do, and she'd be doing it even if we weren't paying her, so don't be an idiot."

The side of me that's been a professional Dom for fifteen years knows that's a very good thing. The rest of me is pissed off and cranky and out of sorts. "I'll find shit that needs repairing today. I probably shouldn't inflict myself on actual people."

"Good to know where I rank," says Damon dryly.

I reach for the stapler to throw at his head, but he beats me to it. He leans back in his chair and raises the eyebrow that says I'd better talk or I'm going to seriously regret it.

I growl at him. "I taught you that look."

"Yes, you did."

Fuck. "I pushed on her last night after we left. Probably too hard. Total joykill on a great night."

He shrugs. "You must have had your reasons."

That's the problem, right there. "I did. I'm just not sure I'm right."

His face is more serious now—but it's the eyes of my friend, not my boss. Waiting with patience and compassion, because in our world, talking is everything, even for two tough guys who run the place.

"Two things. First is that I kind of dragged her into this, because I wanted to play and she's curious enough to have given it a shot. But she was really clear that she doesn't want to live on the edges all the time. She did that with her band. Too much blood." I don't need to say any more than that. We've seen plenty of bleeding in our world.

"So you pulled her into the warm and fuzzy world of kink."

This office needs more staplers. "For her it kind of is. She totally fit in last night, and there's plenty of warm and fuzzy in what we've built here."

It's his turn to scowl. "I blame that part on Ari."

We both know that's bullshit, so I don't bother saying so. It comes straight from the top—she's just the cheerful, cute face we put on it these days so that people don't try to hug us all the time. "Hell, even Emily totally fits in here, and she's way more mainstream than Scorpio."

Damon gets the goopy look in his eyes that happens whenever Emily's name comes up. "Yeah."

I snort. "Focus. You're supposed to be quizzing me on my problems."

He eyes the stapler meaningfully. "I am. So you think Scorpio wants the soft version of our lifestyle, whatever the heck that is."

I don't have to take this shit from my best friend. "Isn't that pretty much what you're giving Emily?"

"It might look that way." He shrugs. "It feels plenty intense."

That's exactly the problem. "I used Ari's porn thing with Scorpio, and I saw something. You know that look subs get when they want something but it's scaring them away?"

He's nodding. "You have to push."

It's one of the basic laws of gravity for what we do. "I did. She pushed back. Called it a hard limit."

He winces. "Fuck. Tread carefully."

I scowl at him. "Why the hell do you think I'm in your office? I've got a sub who wants a few edges with lots of safe landings in between, and I pushed her at an edge too fast and she's telling me to back the hell off. Except her words and her body are saying different things."

Damon's watching me with that revved-up stillness he has. "You have the best instincts in the business. If you think she needs this, then you made a commitment to take her there."

I jam my head in my hands. "I know. So why am I feeling so damn cranky about it?"

The words from the other side of the desk are quiet—and unrelenting. "What do you want to do?"

Crap. I look up, because telling the truth has been the first rule between us since before this office existed. "I want to hold her and tell her she's safe and let that be enough."

He looks at me, and then he smiles, and I can see that all the cards have just hit the table. "Those are the words of a Dom who's falling for his sub."

Those are the words of a man who's falling for a woman. "I blame you. What the fuck door of hell did you open around here?"

He grins. "Don't let Emily hear you say that."

She's not the woman I'm worried about. "I can't think that way about Scorpio. It will mess with all my Dom instincts. It already is."

Damon's grin is just getting bigger. "Sing it, brother."

I want to make his nose bleed, but I'm pretty sure his sub would hurt me. "I manage a sex club. I like my life that way."

He starts humming something under his breath that even I know is a wedding song.

This time the stapler doesn't miss.

Chapter Thirty-Two

SCORPIO

I walk through Fettered's back door and sigh. The man needs to get out more, so that I don't have to keep walking into a sex club to find him. There are edges here, even on a sunny morning when the kitchen smells like Gabby's carrot muffins.

The three guys sitting at the counter eating them all stare at me, and then Damon and Quint mumble about things they need to do and head for the hills. I notice they manage to raid most of the muffins on their way out.

Harlan's looking at me like he can't figure out whether to hold me or spank me. "Hi, beautiful."

I don't want him to be nice to me this morning. I can feel the fight I want to pick with him rising in my throat, and I swallow it down. Ari says he's offering me a gift. Until I can think straight, I'm going to try to believe her. I reach into my pocket and pull out the image that has collected an impressive number of wrinkles and stains since last night. I don't let him see it yet. "I came to talk to you about this."

He looks at me and nods slowly. "Lap or stool?"

I want to crawl into him and stay forever, but there's no

way I'm going to get the words out if I do. I fold my arms over my chest and stand my ground. "You're right. This isn't a hard limit, although I really want to say it is. It's just something about me that I wish you didn't see."

He pats the stool beside him. "Come sit down. Have a muffin. Did Ari make sure you ate something this morning?"

The fight I swallowed is back in full force. "Did you send her?"

"No." He's not dodging my mad at all. "But I would if I thought you needed somebody."

My hands clench into fists. "I'm not fragile."

"I know that." His hand moves toward me and then lands flat on the counter. "I talked to Damon this morning. In this lifestyle, talking is huge, and needing someone to talk to is never a weakness."

He's treading way too close to lands I don't want to visit. "Sorry. I'm in a pissy mood."

"I can see that." He mostly manages to hide his smile. "Have a muffin."

"I don't want a bloody muffin." I slam the image down on the counter. "This is the one."

He's watching me, not the picture.

Fuck. He already knows.

His eyes are gentle, but there's no escaping them. "Why is this the one?"

I want to tell him. I thought I came here to tell him. To trust this big man with the muffin crumbs on his lip and the eyes that care about me —but I can't. Not even for him. And that pisses me off more than anything ever. "I don't know. The lingerie, maybe."

His hand slaps down on the image. "Don't dig yourself in any deeper, beautiful." His other hand turns my chin to face him. "You promised to tell me the truth, even when it gets hard. You're new to this, so I've given you some latitude with not telling me stuff. But don't fucking lie."

I can feel something in me snapping—and I let it. "You don't own me." The words fire out like bullets. Seeking blood.

Chapter Thirty-Three

HARLAN

She's a trembling, snarling mess—and she's not done. "You don't get to demand that I strip every damn thing for you just so you can get some kind of joyride off being a control freak."

Fuck, how do I help her through this?

It's not her words that matter right now. Those are just hot air. She's right on the edge of bolting—and if she does, she won't come back. I know this as surely as I know my own name. And I'm frozen by the war going on between the man and the Dom inside me. The man needs to hold her close and respect the edges she wants to stay away from and tell her it doesn't matter and she's entirely worthy just as she is. The Dom needs to help her be everything. It's why I do this. To help people become who they're supposed to be, let light into their dark places, strip off their armor, find their place to belong.

The Dom can feel the need beating in the woman in front of me, mouthing off so that I won't see her.

But if I push, and I'm going to have to push hard, the chances are really good she's going to run, and I don't know if she'll ever come back. She's given me all kinds of warning—a sub who knows exactly where her quicksand lives and wants to fence it off and keep everyone the hell out.

I fall back on fifteen years of training. I don't know what else to do. I snap as hard into Dom mode as I can, every fragment of body language making it clear what I expect. "There will be punishment for mouthing off, for lying to me. It will arrive in a box at your office in one hour." It would be better to do it right now, but I can't. I need to get a grip on the man first, so he doesn't sabotage everything the Dom knows is right.

I leave the kitchen while she's still speechless, heading for my safe place, for the dungeon that was the center of my world until a few days ago. I know before I make it two steps that leaving her alone like this is the hardest thing I've ever done— but I'm pretty sure it's going to pale against what's coming next.

He's a dead man—and then I'm going to make him rise from the dead so that I can kill him again.

I grab the box that I just opened on my desk, crumple the note that came with it into something the size of a spitball, and storm out of my office. Where I promptly collide with my favorite videographer and dump both of us on our asses. He stares at the maid costume that's now spread out all over the hallway. The very skimpy, porny maid costume.

"Um, dare I ask?"

I growl and park my butt against a wall. "Harlan wants me to wear that. I'm on my way to kill him."

Leo winces and slides his butt to sit against the wall across from me. "The man has balls, I'll give him that."

I can't believe he's even thinking of taking Harlan's side. "This was one of my hard limits."

He looks at the offending white lace again. "What specifically was your limit?"

I stab my finger at the lace. "This. All of this."

He leans forward and rubs a hand down my shin. "Breathe, lady. Details matter here. Was your limit wearing a maid costume, or serving him, or role-play in general, or something else?"

My brain's going to explode. "All of it. Any of it."

He just raises an eyebrow, and I suddenly don't have any doubts at all about what role he plays with Sam. "Do they teach that look at Dom school?"

He flashes me a grin. "Yup."

Figures. "I don't remember our conversation super clearly, but it's the idea of being seen as something less that really torques me."

He nods. "For what it's worth, Sam dresses up in all kinds of things where someone on the outside might assume that, and not once, ever, have I thought he was less than me. Mostly the opposite, but he kicks my butt when I talk that way."

I try to imagine Sam in a maid costume and what's left of my brain falls off a wall of ice into the ocean. "I still don't want to be anyone's servant. Does that make me some kind of judgmental shit?"

The eyebrow is back. "No, it makes you a sub who knows herself well enough to tell her Dom important things that will help keep play safe and fun."

I wince. "Except obviously I wasn't clear enough."

"You're new, and he's the best at reading body language of anyone I know." Leo pats the costume. "Maybe he goofed, and if he did, you'll figure out between you how to clean that up. But unless I'm missing some of the details, it sounds like he asked you to wear it. Not to serve him, not to role play—just to wear it."

I hiss. "I'll feel like less as soon as I put it on."

He leans across the hall and strokes a knuckle down my cheek. "That's very different than being treated as less. I don't know for sure, but it sounds like he's threading a very difficult needle. Doms only do that if they think it's important."

I lift up a leg and kick the door jam. "He wants me to wear it while he spanks me."

Leo's face twitches like hell, but he manages not to laugh. "Fun or punishment?"

Suddenly I'm nauseous and nothing about this feels funny anymore. "Punishment. I lied to him. And I said some really mean, bullshit things. I got scared and I ran off at the mouth and I threw crap at him that he totally didn't deserve."

Leo's arms are around me before I finish speaking, and I turn into him, too upset to be picky about whose chest I whimper on. He holds me while I suck in enough breaths to hold it together, and then he pushes me back up to sitting, his eyes glued to mine. "Better?"

I nod and stay quiet. He's clearly got stuff to say.

"In the vanilla world, when you screw up, you go apologize and then you try to figure out why you did whatever you did so that you don't do it again." He waits until I nod. "In the kink world, with a Dom you trust, punishment can get you there faster and cleaner. It repairs the trust, reminds you both of what you have to lean into so that you don't have to be scared alone the next time."

I can feel the tears forming, and that will end me where I sit, so I choke them back. "Just thinking about it makes me feel like a scared little kid."

"At some point, tell Harlan that. That's the kind of thing your Dom needs to know." He runs a hand down my arm. "In the meantime, know that there's one monumentally important difference between you and that helpless child."

I shake my head at him.

He smiles. "One little word will stop your big man dead in his tracks. You have all the power, lady. Even punishment is your choice."

Chapter Thirty-Five

HARLAN

I'm an idiot. A stuck-in-a-rut idiot who apparently doesn't know how to stop being a Dom even when his happiness depends on it.

I've pushed and now Scorpio's going to run, and then there won't be a wonderful armful of woman in my lap anymore, and even my Dom's not going to be very fucking happy about that. I spin around and head for the door. I spend too damn much of my life in this club and I need to get out.

I make it as far as the front walkway and find Ari sitting on a rock, wrapped up in a scarf and a hat the color of the maple leaves over her head. She takes one look at me and snorts. "Well, it looks like Leo was right."

I don't want to know what Leo has to do with anything. "I'm in no mood to talk."

She twirls a red leaf in her fingers. "That's not your safeword, buddy."

I scowl at her. "Didn't you have breakfast with Scorpio this morning?" There are rules about talking in our lifestyle, but we try hard not to put people in the middle. Even when they're really nosy and volunteer.

She sighs. "Yeah. That makes this a little sticky, but if you talk to one of the guys they might agree with that thick head of yours."

"What are you now, a mind reader?"

"You're thinking you went too hard on her. That you should have backed off." She raises an eyebrow. "How close am I?"

Pretty much on the button, but she doesn't know the half of it. "She came to me this morning. Couldn't get the truth out, so she lied and spewed some nasty crap. I kicked a punishment scene into gear. Sent her a maid costume to wear."

Ari stares at me for a full minute without blinking.

I plunk down on a rock beside her. "So yeah, I'm pretty damn sure I pushed too hard."

She leans into my shoulder. "You've fallen really hard for her, huh?"

I shake her off. "Why the hell is everyone telling me that?"

She snickers and leans back into me. "Remember when Emily came to see Damon in the dungeon? The second time, when she waltzed right in and dared him to spank her?"

Nobody at Fettered will ever forget that—or the scene that came after, where they both put their hearts on naked display for everyone to see. "Emily still doesn't know we were there the next night, does she?"

Ari shakes her head. "We'll tell her when she asks."

I know where she's going with this. "Not all big gambles pay off. What if Scorpio walks?"

"Then you grovel and you fix it." She touches my cheek. "You're not just her Dom, big guy, and she knows that. Trust her. Trust that what the two of you are building together will survive this moment."

I let my head tilt down to her shoulder. "It could be really bad."

She nods her head slowly against my cheek and wraps two warm arms around my middle. "I know."

Chapter Thirty-Six

SCORPIO

If looks could kill, every living thing between my apartment and Fettered would be dead.

I can't believe I'm here.

I stomp up the front stairs—I'm not going in the damn servant entrance. Not dressed like this. The door opens before I can kick it in, which sucks, because I need to take my temper out on something. I don't give a damn if I'm the first maid ever to wear steel-toed boots. Maybe I'll start a trend.

Right after I set Seattle on fire with my eyes.

I know why I'm angry. I know it's a cover for hurt and shame and a dozen other things I don't want to be feeling. Ari and Leo almost had me convinced there's purpose in this, that Harlan's doing it to give me a chance to be something more. Something that doesn't have a tourist bone in its entire body.

They didn't see how I look in this fucking maid gear.

The lounge is empty when I storm through it. I'm not surprised. I warned Ari I was coming.

I shove the dungeon door open and that's where I find him. Standing in the middle of his domain, in leathers that say just how long he's lived here. Waiting for me to show up and grovel.

If that's what he wanted, he left way too many loopholes in his instructions. I'm following them. To the letter. And not a damn hair more.

I stop a foot from his nose. I refuse to be scared of this.

I shake off the trench coat I borrowed from Leo and dare him to say a word. His stupid note didn't say anything about walking here dressed like a freaking porn extra. Clearly he went out of his way to find the most revealing maid getup in the history of the universe—and then bought it a size too small to spite me.

Edges. Blood. Today I want it to be his.

He doesn't laugh. He doesn't even ogle my boobs, and this getup doesn't leave much of them covered. He just studies me with silent, serious eyes. When he finally speaks, his voice is quiet. "Why are you here?"

I wonder if he's ever been kicked in the balls. I'm here, I'm furious, and I did what he asked. He just needs to fucking get on with it. "For my spanking."

"For your punishment."

I will not crawl. "Call it whatever you like."

He backs slowly over to the same spanking bench we used yesterday and sits down. "Come here."

There's no sign of softness. No sign of the man who did this so playfully last night while everyone listened. "No." My anger is gone, a freaking bloody coward that fled the moment he spoke. I can't do this.

His eyes are uncompromising granite. "That's not your safeword. Use it or get your ass over my knee."

Lightning. I'm going to say it. I intend to say it. I open my mouth to say it—and then I start shaking like a leaf, because somewhere in here is an edge I need and I don't know how to leave without it and I don't know how to stay.

Chapter Thirty-Seven
HARLAN

So close. So fucking close and I almost lost her and now I need to honor the fuck out of her choosing to stay, even if she doesn't know it yet.

I do the work she can't. I get her sexy ass bare and bent over my knee, make sure her face is comfortable on the spanking bench, because she's going to go way deep now and I need to take her there and take amazing care of what she's about to do and be.

I run my hand over her ass, letting her feel me. I can see the stunned look on her face. Her brain's totally shut down. The rest of her is trusting me to get this right.

She whimpers as my hand lands on her ass, and it's still sounding mostly scared. I can't let that be where she goes. I pick up the rhythm, splintering the last of her resistance and giving somewhere for the shattered pieces to go. She's absolutely silent for long enough to worry me—and then something in her releases on a long, aching cry of relief, and her ass reaches for the next swing of my hand.

My sub has found her surrender.

I give her exactly what she needs. Freedom. My hand

raining down absolution on her ass. The reminder that she can go scary places and do scary things and find the woman she wants to be out the other side. The hard, sharp knowing that sometimes fire is the best way through.

I feel her riding it—and then I feel her let go. Beyond sensation, past surrender.

I gentle things slowly so that whatever part of her is still tuned into my hand gets the chance it needs to exhale.

My touch, her heartbeat. And then, when she's done, I pick her up and turn her gently over and find the big armchair where we can sit forever if we need to.

My legs try to protest the walk there, but I don't let them. I'll shake later. Right now everything I am is for her.

I sit down, and I hold her in tight to my chest, and I breathe in the smell of trust and shattering and doing hard things. She shudders, and I snug her in tighter to my heartbeat. I'm not a Dom who's afraid of earthquakes, and she needs to know I'll hold her while she shakes. For as long as it takes.

I'm so fucking grateful she's here.

Chapter Thirty-Eight

SCORPIO

I don't know how long I'm in the timeless place. Ari's told me about it. Subspace. She says it's better than orgasm.

She's wrong. It's in an entirely different galaxy.

This is peace, like the kind that comes when three notes in a song find each other and the whole world stops to listen. The place where holy exists and absolute rightness is totally a thing and humanity divides into people who get it and people who don't.

The man who has wrapped his whole body around me brought me here. Turned my fire and brimstone into something so beautiful I can't stand it—and I can't leave.

I don't know if the sound under my ear is his heartbeat or mine. It doesn't matter. It's the sound of utter safety, of a promise so vast I had no idea what it meant until now.

I almost walked away from this.

I'd kick myself all over hell for that, but the peace of here would never allow that—and neither will the man who gave me this.

He faced my anger, my fury, my impending flight. He made me face them too. Now it's time to thank him.

As soon as I find the part of me that knows how to speak.

Chapter Thirty-Nine

HARLAN

She's coming back to me. One heartbeat at a time—and her body is the liquid calm of a sub who has totally gone through something huge and come out the other side.

It's me who needs to shake. I almost lost her.

I pull her in tighter to my naked chest. She might not need it. I do.

She runs her fingers over the lace of the only maid uniform I could find on really short notice. "You used this to get past my crap."

That she can see that, even as she sits totally wasted in my lap, is like magic oil for my heart. I take my first really solid breath in hours. The man needs her to hear what the Dom would never say. "I was scared you wouldn't come."

She's rubbing her cheek on my chest like it's all that's holding her to the world. "Leo helped me."

The list of people I owe on this is getting ridiculous. "I'm glad he was there for you. For us."

She nods.

I tune into her breathing, her muscle tone, her heartbeat. Sub calm and aware, and clueless about where she might have left her armor. It's time to finish this. I slide the grimy, stained picture that has caused such grief onto her lap. "Talk to me, beautiful."

Her fingers trace over the lines that have formed in the picture. "The lingerie is a symbol, somehow. Of what her eyes are saying. Wearing on the outside what she's feeling on the inside."

I kiss her hair. We both know plenty about making statements with our outsides. "What do you see in her eyes?"

She shakes again, but these are the good kind. "I want to say weakness, because when I'm scared, that's what it looks like. But it's not. It's softness."

Now we've hit truth. Deep, beautiful rivers of it. I stroke her hair and let it soak into both of us.

She pushes herself off my chest, but she isn't backing away. She's seeking my eyes. "I need to say this before I get scared again. I want soft. I want cuddles and candlelight and to be taken care of. Not all the time, but some of the time, and I'm scared that you'll think I'm weak if I need those things. That I'll think I'm weak. And I'm scared of what will happen if I say I need those things and then open up for them and they aren't there." She blew out a breath. "Music used to open me up like that, but there wasn't any safe place to be soft."

Because no one expects a chick in black and chains to need tenderness.

I cup my hands around the face of my gorgeous sub who wants to be surrender that isn't weak. I kiss her forehead, her cheeks, the cold tip of her nose. "Beautiful, I'm a Dom. I live to hear that the woman in my arms wants those things." I tip back her head, brush my thumb down the curve of her neck. "It's not weakness. It's not even softness. You want to be cherished."

Tears fill her eyes and spill down her cheeks and I don't

think she even knows they're there. She's too busy letting a single word sink in and reshape the hidden thing, the shameful thing, into something that can live in the light. I cuddle her into me, needing to feel her everywhere. Needing to hold her while she reforms.

She wants to be cherished.

Doing that job right will take more than man or Dom has ever given.

Chapter Forty

SCORPIO

Cherished. It's like he's yanked all the clothes off the part of me that I thought was scarred and ugly and made me look and see that it's not ugly at all.

I stare down at a crinkled, abused photograph, and suddenly it's all I can see.

Cherished.

Something that can only happen if I'm willing to be soft. I huff in a breath. "Ari looked like this. At charades night when she peeled off her pants and stood there looking all ravishable."

I can hear the low, proud growl above my head. "Yeah. She did."

I won't be that brave in a thousand years of trying. "How does she do that? Be so open and so tough all at the same time?"

Harlan shifts us in the big chair so that I can see his eyes and lays his hand under my cheek. "I don't know. But this is about you, not about her. You have that same need to be tough and to be vulnerable."

Even that word is scary. "How the hell do I do that?"

He grins. "In the vanilla world, I have no idea. In this one, you trust me to give you what you need."

I can feel my body trying to squiggle back from him.

He stops me with a snort and a kiss to my forehead.

My brain kicks into gear, since clearly my body is a total pushover. "So like the shrinky-dink flogger—that's part of giving me space to be brave and tough, right?"

He's laughing. "Shrinky-dink?"

I poke his ribs. "You know the one I mean. The hot-rain one." I flutter my eyelashes at him. "That I hope you use again soon."

He shakes his head and glares, but I can see the amusement in his eyes. "You know what we call subs like you, right?"

I grin. "Yup. Brat." Based on what I saw at charades night, I'm going to have to work if I want to earn that title.

He leans in and kisses me, and it makes all my non-bratty parts go soft and gooey. "Yeah, things like sensation play, impact stuff, anything that pushes you towards pain lines, those are all ways a sub can breathe into her own power."

I remember how I felt after the hot rain. "I like that part."

He touches a finger to my nose. "You also find it easier than most subs, because that's power you already know how to wear well, inside and outside."

I trace a finger down his tats. I'm not the only one. I can also hear where this is going, and the part of me that's tough decides to get there first. "So basically I'm weird because I like a flogger and I'm scared of lingerie."

He chuckles. "Weird doesn't have much meaning in this lifestyle." He pauses, and his eyes look so deep into mine. "What it means is that things that look soft or vulnerable or weak are sharper edges for you. It will take more trust between us for you to find your surrender in those ways."

I eye him suspiciously. "I'm not a big fan of punishment as a trust-building exercise."

He groans and squeezes me tighter. "Me neither."

I snuggle in a little closer, because I can see that he really means it. "The in-between after doesn't suck, though."

He's breathing me in, his hand running up and down my back. Soaking in this gift he's given us, because Ari and Leo were totally right about that part. "You're not going to stop pushing on me about this, are you." I don't make it a question —it totally isn't. More of a pout, really.

The rumbling laughter under my ear isn't an answer.

It's a promise.

Chapter Forty-One
SCORPIO

Friday morning, and miracle of all miracles, we don't have any weddings this weekend. Which should make this meeting really short. I slide into the seat beside Leo and sigh gratefully. "I love fall. Nothing to do."

He grins and leans into my shoulder. "Want to help edit video?"

My job ends about six hours after a wedding is done. His rolls on for weeks, especially when we're coming out of the slammed end-of-summer season. "Sure. Can I pick music, too?"

He snorts and fills my coffee. "Not a chance."

I pretend to pout. "You let me do Doxy and Jimmy's video."

"Exactly." He casts me a careful look, under the guise of slurping his own coffee. "How are you?"

There are some things even I can't manage to talk about at work, but he helped me out in ways I'm only beginning to understand, and he deserves an answer. "I showed up. I almost safeworded out."

He breathes slowly into his mug. "It doesn't get much bigger than that."

"Mountains moved. Some of them might still be moving."

His hand runs down my forearm. "He'll need you today."

"I've been wondering about that." I put my hand over his. Leo's been a really good friend through this, and clearly he's not done yet. Screw work and privacy. I need to know. "Have you and Sam ever done anything like that? A punishment thing?"

"Yeah." He sighs, and the look on his face is so stinking happy it nearly kills me. "Sam asked me to marry him two days later."

Whoa. I pick up my coffee cup, trying not to look horrified.

He laughs, right from his belly to his snazzy hair. "Don't worry, I don't think it's contagious."

I elbow him, trying to process what he's just told me. My brain cells aren't firing in high gear today. I think some of them decided to take a vacation somewhere between subspace and Harlan's hand. "You're telling me it's going to change things between us."

"Nope." He leans over and kisses my forehead. "I'm telling you it already has."

"Cut that out, you two." Emily walks in, rolling her eyes. "No kissing at work."

Leo stands up and plants one right on her lips. "We love you too, boss lady."

She backs away from him, holding up a folder to ward him off, but she's smiling while she does it. "I have no idea what's in the water around here lately."

I snort. Like hell she doesn't. "You totally started it."

She blushes, and it's pretty darn clear her imagination has taken that remark and run with it.

Leo hides a grin and pulls out a chair for Gabby, who has just walked in and noticed all the energy zinging around the room. She blinks at each one of us in turn and then takes a seat. "Is everyone ready for the charity ball tonight?"

I stare at her.

Leo takes one look at my face and nearly snorts coffee out his nose. "You forgot, didn't you?"

Gabby looks horrified. "You need a dress." She turns to Emily, appeal written on every line of her face. "All the weddings are in fine shape—please tell me we can take Scorpio shopping."

This is going to be entirely out of control in about another millisecond. I hold up both hands. "Stop right there, people. Nobody's dressing me up for this thing." I'm not even sure I should go. I have shit to figure out before I walk into Harlan's world again. Especially in anything resembling a dress.

Gabby and Emily both start talking at the same time—but it's Leo who gets my attention, quietly and very insistently. His hand is back on my arm, and this time I can feel the Dom in him. "He'll need you there. Whatever you need to figure out, do it with him."

I glare at him, but there's no heat in it. "I so need to have a chat with Sam."

He leans back, devilment in his eyes. "He'd love to take you shopping."

Gods. "Shopping doesn't fix anything in my world, no matter what the rest of you think."

Gabby looks like she wants to distract me with cookies until the nice men with the little white pills get here. "I don't mind helping you, if you want. Leo found me this beautiful purple dress. It's retro and it curves in all the places I do and I can't wait for you to see it."

Cripes. I can't let her go alone. She's way too freaking

sweet and edible. "I'll find something, okay?" I have a whole closet full of punk-rocker stage gear that would make Ari drool if she ever laid eyes on it. Something in there will work.

I'll slide the skin of the old Scorpio over top of the one who got birthed in Harlan's lap yesterday.

Just until I figure out who she is.

Chapter Forty-Two

HARLAN

I feel like a Martian at a football game. This place even smells like somewhere I don't belong.

I scowl at the perky woman in pink headed my way. There's just no way I need help from anyone who looks that cheerfully annoying. I give her a look that would have any sub at Fettered scampering the other way.

She keeps coming, entirely unfazed by the thunderclouds on my face. "Hello, and welcome to Pretty Things, Seattle's best boutique lingerie store. Do you need something for the special lady in your life?"

I can't even begin to answer that. "I'll just look around, thanks."

She looks like she might cry any minute. "We pride ourselves on helping you pick out just the right option. Can you tell me a little about her? Size, modesty preferences, favorite colors?"

I know exactly how Scorpio likes to be spanked—and I don't know her favorite color. I shift uneasily, wondering just how fast I can get to the door.

"Mandy, take a break. I'll be happy to help out this gentleman."

The voice behind me is cool, clear water—and obviously one the woman in front of me knows better than to disobey. Mandy shoots me one last pouty look and scoots, right out the front door of the store.

I turn to face my savior. She's about my age, beautiful in a way that doesn't remotely translate into pretty, and not making any effort at all to hide her amusement. "Sorry. Mandy's a wonder with nervous brides, but she doesn't have any idea what to do with a big man who just panicked."

I have a rep to maintain. "I didn't panic. Quite."

She laughs, and it matches the rest of her. Classy, confident, and not remotely stuck up. "I'm Chloe, and I'll help you get out of here before Mandy is back from her break."

I glance around. "This your place?"

"Yes." She nods at a big chair in the corner. "Sit there and we'll chat."

I drag my feet over to the place clearly designed for clods like me. "Looks like you've done this before."

"A few times." She's got the whole calm-expert thing down to perfection. "Tell me about the person you're shopping for."

Someone who wouldn't feel any more at home in this very vanilla lingerie store than I do. "She's vibrant, alternative, slender, likes to be noticed."

Her eyebrow goes up. "You're observant."

So is she, but she probably thinks of that as her job. "What else do you need to know?"

She flashes a grin, and in that moment there's a lot more to Chloe than a classic exterior. "You want something she'll wear underneath, something to sleep in, or something to peel off?"

Damn, I like her. "Isn't it all supposed to peel off?"

She swoons, hand over her heart, and then winks at me. "Don't move."

I watch her flit, a bird landing in the pretties and lifting off again—one who knows exactly what she wants. She's back in a couple of minutes, and I'm deeply grateful to see only a few choices in her arms. She's not expecting me to winnow through half the store.

She holds up a long, purple sheath. "Sleek, with just a hint of lace." She holds it out for me to feel. "The silk's nice and thick, and it's totally yummy to wear."

I know quality when I feel it. I also know my sub doesn't get to cover herself up nearly that much. Not if I'm choosing, anyhow. "There needs to be less of it."

She chuckles and reaches for a second hanger. This one is a dark-teal teddy and far skimpier. "The woman who makes these for me is local, and I could live in this lace. Nice and stretchy and very soft."

And very see-through, which almost has me saying yes, because I can totally imagine the outlines of Scorpio's nipples and the texture of the lace between my hands and her skin. But Chloe is stopping me—not with her words, but with her carefully contained certainty that whatever she still has in her pile is the best choice.

I know better than to argue with that. "I like this. Now show me the one you think I should pick."

I've surprised her, and she lets me see it. "This last one is more about her than about you."

Which is why she gave me the chance to pick see-through lace first. "That's what I'm here for."

She holds up her last selection and I know she's utterly, totally nailed it. She puts it in my lap and lets go, like she already knows it's gone. "Cami and boy shorts, and probably the nicest feel of anything I have in my store."

It's deep purple, with a wide band of black lace that will wrap Scorpio's breasts and silky straps that will slide off with a breath and panties loose enough to give me easy access. It will tuck away under whatever armor she wants to wear in the world. A hidden layer only the two of us know about.

That pleases the hell out of man and Dom.

Chapter Forty-Three
SCORPIO

I can hear him walking up the stairs to my office. I stare at the text on my phone that invited him here, stupidly happy that he came, and very glad everyone else has taken off to start their primping for tonight.

I need to be alone with the man who totally rocked my world.

I watch him as he comes into view in my doorway, and I can't decide whether to launch myself at him or hide under my desk. I'm some new kind of naked with him that I suspect isn't ever going to go away, and it's making me shy.

He smiles and comes over and sits in my sad excuse for a guest chair. "Hi."

That totally isn't going to work. I get up and navigate the piles that will get me to his lap, well aware I've got a goopy grin on my face that I can't seem to turn off.

His arms are up and reaching for me before I land. Which is how I end up straddled over his lap instead of whatever ill-formed thing I had planned. I blink and grin at him as he drops me squarely on top of his erection and holds me tight. "Hi, yourself."

He slides a hand under my shirt and cops himself a feel while he nuzzles into my neck.

I kiss along his jawline to his mouth, because the order of the stuff we've done together is seriously weird and we somehow mostly skipped this part. I nibble on his lower lip, licking up tiny tastes of him.

He groans and runs his hands up into my hair, but he doesn't take control.

I'm the one who pulls his head in, deepens the kiss, asks for more of the fire he's leashing. I can feel his cock hot and hard against my pussy and I grind into him.

He puts both hands on my ass and pulls me even tighter against him, and for one wild moment I feel who Harlan will be when he finally lets go. And then he's tipping his forehead into my shoulder, stroking my back, quivering a little as he brings us both back to somewhere that's clearly not headed for fast, hard sex on my office floor.

I push off his chest a little and punch him in the shoulder. "That was mean."

He brushes some hair back behind my ear. "You started it."

And nearly set loose an inferno. "Why'd you stop?"

He just looks at me for a minute, drinking me in, and I can hear that his breath is still hitching some.

I keep my smile to myself. My Dom isn't as calm and cool as he wants me to believe. Somehow it makes me feel better to know he's torturing us both. I lean in and bite his earlobe, and grin when his whole body twitches. "Someday soon, I hope you don't."

His hands tighten on my ass.

I squirm, because that part of me is still tender from last night.

He chuckles and rubs his hands in easy circles. "Sore?"

I have no idea how a question like that feels so intimate, but it does. "A little." I tilt my head down. "I don't mind."

He tips my chin up until I meet his eyes. Asking, so gently, for the rest of it.

Damn him. "It helps me remember what it felt like yesterday. After." When I tried to meld myself into his chest and never leave. I trace a finger over a seam of his t-shirt, so not used to feeling this shy. "Will we do stuff like that a lot?"

He blows out a quick breath and smiles at me. "Hell, no." His hands run down my shoulders. "Punishment's a big thing for some Doms, but I'm not one of them. Only when it feels like the best way through a big blockade, and I don't think you have very many of those."

His words are resonating with something I already know. "And next time I'll trust you faster."

The vulnerable, pleased look on his face nearly melts me where I sit.

I run my fingers along his jawbone, needing to touch. Needing to find the shape of whatever this is between us. "So what brings you to my office in the middle of the day?"

He rubs his chin against my hand. "You texted me. And I brought you a present."

That has alarm bells going off fast and loud. I lean back far enough to give him the evil eye.

He laughs and reaches for bag on the floor that I never saw come in. I eye the elegant silver lettering on a cranberry background with every ounce of suspicion I possess. "That looks like something you should be giving to Emily. Or Gabby. Or anyone who isn't me."

He puts it on his lap between us, and his eyes are still holding the echoes of vulnerable.

Shit. Whatever this is, it's big. I reach into the bag, trying not to wince as I run into silk and lace. If this is another maid costume I'm killing him dead where he sits, no matter what his eyes are saying.

He doesn't say a word as I pull the lingerie out and let it run over my fingers. Some sort of cami with thin straps and black lace and purple silk. I try to swallow and discover I can't. "It's actually pretty nice."

His laughter shakes both of us. "There's a bottom in there too. Something called boy shorts."

He's pushing on me again, and I want to push back—but I can't. He went shopping for me. I try to imagine Harlan in a lingerie store and my mind can't compute. "Are there any dead sales ladies I need to know about?"

He grins. "Nope. I got saved by the owner. She chased away all the scary minions."

Smart woman. I let myself finger the lace a little. I know what he's asking of me, this man who sits me in his lap and takes so little and gives so much. "You want me to wear this for you."

"Nope." He brushes my cheek with his thumb. "I'd like you to wear it for you. Maybe under whatever you're wearing to the dance tonight."

It isn't just for me. I'm not the only one who shifted somewhere new yesterday. It's in his eyes.

None of which means I have to go down easy. I lift an eyebrow. "Maybe on another planet where retired punk-rock singers can be bribed."

He grins, and there's more than a little dangerous in it. "Oh, I brought bribery too." He reaches into his pocket and pulls out the vibrating egg that spent a memorable interlude in my butt. "Turn around, drop your jeans, and point that luscious ass at me."

I'm gaping, because this is totally my Dom and I didn't even see him coming. "This is my office." My empty office, but I have to have some kind of line in the sand.

He kisses my nose. "Now, beautiful."

Chapter Forty-Four

HARLAN

The sparks in her eyes are gorgeous. She's aroused and embarrassed and slightly defiant, and she's letting me see it all. I reach for one of her nipples and squeeze it. "If you do it fast, I'll take out the butt plug once I'm done playing with your pussy. If you do it slow, you'll be dancing with it in tonight."

I totally win either way, and so does she.

She groans, but she's already climbing off my lap, her cheeks flushed and her eyes wanting. She turns around and undoes her belt, slowly enough that I know she's messing with me, and just fast enough to keep me from doing anything about it. Her pants hit the floor, and then she's shimmying off her silky black panties and it's all I can do to keep my tongue in my head.

Instead, I get smart this time and help her out of her pants and boots. Then I put my hand on her lower back. "Bend over. Hands on your desk."

She does, and the sight of her, all wet and slick and open to me, is enough to stretch my control to the very edges. The only thing that holds me back is knowing that it would be the first time I slide my cock into her, and this isn't the way I've planned it.

This is just foreplay.

I wrap my hands around her thighs and move to the front of my chair and lick my tongue all the way from her clit to the valley between her ass cheeks, and the taste of her scrambles every coherent thought I have left.

She moans and leans back into my face.

I lick again, exploring her more fully this time, moving my fingers up to pull her even more open for me.

She shudders, and I can tell her legs aren't going to hold her up for much of this. I consider dumping her on her back on her desk, but it's got more piles on it than I've ever seen in one place, and it's probably not fair to make her come all over next week's work.

I quiet my tongue, soothing her with my fingers while I pull some lube out of my back pocket. I slick up the plug and her ass at the same time, adding some of the juice from her pussy that smells so much better than anything that ever came out of a bottle.

I slide a finger into her ass, and when I can feel how relaxed she is, I switch it out for the plug. I need some help from her to get it in from this position, and she leans back into my pressure like a pro. I turn it gently, easing it in, not letting her take it any faster than she can easily handle. This is all about pleasure.

When it slides into place, I bend in again and lick her pussy, reveling in the taste and smell of her. There's going to be so much more of this in my not-very-distant future, but not right now. My sub's legs are done. "In my lap. Straddling me like you were before."

She's there so fast I barely have time to catch her, her eyes wide and glistening and fiercely ready.

I wrap one hand around the back of her neck and, with the other, slide two fingers into her pussy and start a hard, fast beat against the spot that I already know sends her up rocket fast. Her eyes never leave mine, even as she starts to moan and whimper and her focus totally hazes.

She pushes into both my hands as she arches, reaching for the edge I'm sending her to with every gorgeous, intense cell of who she is. I move my fingers faster inside her and brush my thumb over her clit. "That's it. Come for me, beautiful."

She does, in hot, wet spurts all over my hand.

I grin and reach into my pocket and pull out the vibrator remote. I wait just long enough for her to register what it is, long enough to get my other thumb right where I want it over her clit, and then I push the button.

Her forehead lands on my shoulder as she absolutely shatters, blown into the lands where one orgasm doesn't separate itself from the next. She rocks fiercely on my hand, even as I turn off the vibrator, needing nothing from me now except the certainty that I am holding her.

I let her ride until her rocking slows under its own steam, bringing her down to exactly the landing she wants. The panting in my ear shifts to whispering, reverent sighs, and I wrap my free hand around her and snug her into my chest as best as I can without taking away the fingers she's still riding.

This went somewhere deeper than a plug in her ass and a quick feel at work, and I do it the honor of looking it square in the eyes and naming what I see.

There's a door wide open between us.

Tonight we'll see what walks through.

Chapter Forty-Five

SCORPIO

I sit on my bed, buck naked, the sounds of my favorite bad-ass playlist pounding the walls of my apartment, and sigh. Even classic rock can't pull me out of this weird place I've landed in.

I sigh again and turn off the music. Time to hear myself think.

There are clothes all over my apartment. I've emptied my closet and the spare-bedroom one that holds my retired performance gear, and I've found three dozen things I could wear to the dance. All of them would probably work, because, charity ball or not, this is a Fettered event and black, chains, and leather are never going to be outside the lines.

But I can't do it.

I finger the lingerie that's been sitting on the end of my bed for the last two hours, staring at me and daring me and keeping me honest.

Last time Harlan sent me something to wear, I went to him full of anger and fury and darkness. This time he's asking me to show up as my softest self—and he's giving me an out. The option to hide it under whatever else I'm wearing tonight. To wear purple and lace for him and for me, and to be some comfortable version of Scorpio for everyone else.

He's willing to let me hide. The man who's favorite kink is public, and whose family will be at this dance.

I flop back on my bed, annoyed and uncomfortable because in two closets' worth of stuff, nothing is close to what I need. I have fifteen pairs of army boots and not a single pair of dancing shoes, and that just drives home the message of the spanking that landed on my ass last night.

Somewhere along the way, I've gotten way too comfortable being tough.

I look at the two options on the foot of my bed that are the best choices I can find inside the four walls of my apartment. The first one is a dress I wore to Freddy's wedding. It's black and silky and a little bit frilly, and it fits the bill for what to wear tonight better than anything else I own.

Except for the fact that Freddy's a coke-addicted asshole now and his wedding is divorce-streaked dust.

I don't want to carry blood in with me tonight.

My second option is the only other dress I own. It's short, sleek, and black with a fishnet overlay, and it goes great with army boots. All the Dommes would be jealous. Which is so not the way I want to feel tonight.

I growl at both options and pitch them into my monstrous discard pile. When did my clothes become my armor? When did I get this scared of being a human being who is soft and bleeds and is willing to let people see that?

And what do I do with the man who was willing to hold up that mirror for me even as I hissed and clawed at him?

I close my eyes and see his face in my office. The one that showed up asking for my trust. The vulnerable heart that lives beneath the leathers. That's the man I need to dress for tonight. For him and for the woman he's somehow made the space for me to want to be.

I laugh, and feel the energy of rightness billowing to life inside me. I know what I need to do. What I want to do.

I have two hours. It's time to prove just how good I am at back-room miracles.

Chapter Forty-Six

HARLAN

"Holy shit. Harlan?"

I turn and scowl at the evil grin of the man behind me. "Shut up."

The woman beside him smiles at me, delighted. "Ignore him. You look totally handsome."

I feel like a walrus that got lost and can't find his way back to the sea. "It's a dance. Ari said to dress up."

Emily's eyes are twinkling. "Okay. You stick with that story."

I shake my head at her. "Since when did you get all wise and tough and gorgeous?" She's in something yellow and shiny that lights her up like the sun.

Damon growls and tugs her in closer. "Go find your own woman."

I'm trying, but she's not here yet.

Emily's eyes get wide. "Uh, sweetie—I think the mayor just walked in."

We all blink—he's kink friendly, but generally in a distant, hands-off kind of way. Apparently a nice hotel ballroom has changed his policy some. I watch as my best friend and his personal sunshine head off on an intercept course, and wonder what the heck I'm supposed to do with myself.

I try to stuff my hands in my pockets, but fancy jackets clearly aren't meant to make that possible. I scowl and check out the ballroom instead. It's big and pretty and the people dancing in the middle look happy, so I assume Ari has pulled off another of her decorating miracles.

Fettered's membership is here in force, but they've heeded the request to be visible and interesting, but not outrageous. Which is clearly stretching some of them, and I can totally sympathize. I'm a Dom way out of his dungeon.

Ari swings by, dancing with the man who handled her so well at charades night. It's too bad he's just visiting. I let myself feel sad for her, even though she'd poke me in the ribs for it. Ari's amazing, and there aren't enough Doms who can truly partner her when she wants to surrender.

"It's going to suck for her when he leaves." Quint's at my shoulder, watching the same pair of dancers.

"Yeah." I look over at him, measuring. "She's kind of screwed when all the best Doms in Seattle think of her as their little sister."

He snorts. "I'm not fucking playing with Ari. Get your mind out of the gutter."

"Just checking." The rest of us have been a dead loss for years.

"I love her and I'll take apart any guy who messes with her, and that's where it ends."

He'll have to get in line. "She's pretty good at taking care of herself." Which is part of the problem. Finding a guy who can handle all of who she is won't be an easy job.

Maybe not all that different from the one I've suddenly landed in.

"Ari's not the only one I'm keeping my eye on tonight." Quint points his chin at the woman who mans the front desk at Your Perfect Moment. "There's some interest brewing there."

Gabby's dancing with Jacob, smiling up at him sweetly. "He's way taken. Marla doesn't share."

Quint's shaking his head. "She's being smart and dancing with guys who are safe. But she's starting to wonder what we do behind closed doors."

I stare at him and then at the curvy woman on the dance floor who's blushing furiously at whatever Marla has just said on her way by. "Gabby wants to play?"

"Maybe."

Shit. We've all kind of adopted her as our sweet, sexy, cookie-baking older sister. "Didn't see that one coming." I don't ask if he's sure. Quint's job is new-member intake, and he has that job for a reason. "Does Ari know? Or Emily, maybe?"

"Huh. That's a good idea." Quint starts scanning the ballroom, looking for the woman who's wrapped our boss around her little finger and several other body parts. "I'll get on that. You find Gabby some potential playmates."

I give him a dirty look, even though I'm already running through the member list in my head. Probably not what I'm supposed to be doing at a charity ball, but at least Quint's pulled my head out of my ass some. A little dungeon talk and I'm not feeling quite so fish out of water anymore.

I see movement over by the entry archway, the whispers and murmurs and energy swirls that mean someone special has arrived.

I know who it is. I don't need the speculative looks my direction, or Leo's appreciative whistle, or the stunned glee on Ari's face as she does an excellent impression of a human pogo stick.

I stand still, my heart doing something stupid in my chest, and wait for my woman to arrive. I won't deny her the grand entrance she deserves—or save her from it.

The crowd parts, and it's all I can do not to scoop her up and eat her whole.

She walks toward me slowly, a gift in black and gold and shining eyes.

I try to drink it all in. She's wearing a dress that looks like it fell out of an eighty-year-old movie. Simple and gold with a slit up the front that's giving me glimpses of some very sexy legs and letting the whole damn world see what a glorious hip wiggle she has. Her hair is spilling down around her shoulders, soft and curly and begging for my hands.

But the part that's stabbed me somewhere essential to breathing is the tiny straps of her dress and the plunging neckline that show off the black lace she's wearing underneath. Wearing—and letting everyone see.

She stops a couple of steps away from me, and I'm not the only one staring.

It's Scorpio who finally finds her voice. "Wow. We clean up okay."

Way beyond okay. "You wore it."

She grins at me, but I can see the anxiety dancing in her eyes. "You asked nicely."

I growl, because my Dom wants in on this gig and he's not in the mood to be nice. "You look totally fucking gorgeous. And lickable."

The nerves in her eyes flee, and she laughs.

I hold out my arms, because everything in me is running out of oxygen and I need to hold her. "Dance with me?"

She grins as she steps into my chest. "I probably should have warned you—I can't dance."

I swoop her in, because there's no excuse on Earth that's going to stop me from holding her. "Want to stand on my feet? Ari's been giving me lessons."

Chapter Forty-Seven

SCORPIO

I step into his arms, needing a moment to figure out the rules of gravity on this new planet where we're not at the club and the only leather and chains are on other people.

He wraps me up like I'm everything that's precious, and if I don't know how to dance, I can't remember that anymore. I feel tilted, giddy, off balance and not at all unhappy to be there. He nuzzles into my neck. "With the fancy shoes, you're almost as tall as I am."

The shoes are going to kill me dead, along with the sappy music that's making me want to melt into him and never come back out. "Enjoy them while they last. I'm going to lead a bare-foot revolution in this place in about ten minutes." Club members got warned to stay suitably clothed, but nobody said a word about footwear.

Leo and Sam dance by us, and Sam waggles his eyebrows outrageously. "Scorpio, when you're done with him, can he marry me?"

Harlan snorts. "Someone's angling for a spanking."

"Nope." Sam grins. "I get to flirt with one gorgeous man a night, and you're it, handsome."

I look at Leo and laugh. "How do you keep him alive?"

He shakes his head ruefully. "I have no idea." He neatly navigates Sam between two swirling couples and away.

Harlan growls into my hair, and I just grin. He can play all the Dom cards he wants, but he can't fool me. Something entirely different is flowing here tonight—and I want it, so much more than I ever could have imagined. I want him, but it's not just sex and I don't just want to be his sub. I want what I asked him for before I ever signed his contract, even though I didn't really know the fullness of what I meant. The in-betweens. The time between the edges.

And I'm dancing in the arms of a man who has invited, teased, cajoled, and spanked me into being brave enough to ask for what I want.

But there's something I need to do first, because he's also taught me the power of listening—and I'm hearing so many things from him tonight. I lean into his chest, feeling the strange lines of his crisp, sexy suit under my cheek. A hell of a statement from the man who normally dresses his soft heart in tats and leathers, and I know damn well he's done it for me. To keep me company in my bravery. To be the wind and the Dom and the man at my back.

But maybe for more than that too, and that's the piece I need to chase. I tip my head up to look at him, and the deep happiness in his eyes drowns all my words.

He leans down and kisses me, soft and slow and lazy, like there's all the time in the world. "What is it, beautiful?"

It takes me a moment to remember. I raise a hand to his cheek. "What do you want, Harlan?"

He tips his head, adorably confused.

That's because I'm not making any sense, which is totally the fault of his hands and his eyes and his huge beating heart. "You keep asking me what I want, and giving me that and more I didn't even know I wanted. But you've never really answered that question for me."

His hand tangles gently in my curls. "I'm not clear on all of it yet. Some different things than I wanted a week ago, for sure."

I blow out softly. "Yeah. That makes two of us."

He tips his forehead into mine. "I want more of this."

I can't hold in the smile. "Really? More time in a suit with me stepping on your toes?"

"Ah, you're a lightweight." He grins and kisses my nose. "But yeah. Maybe not the suit. But more time out of the club with you in my arms all soft and pretty—that would be pretty damn awesome."

I give him the evil eye, which actually takes some effort, given my current goopy mood. "I can't believe you just called me pretty. Take it back or I'll go find Mari and feed her some lines about Fettered's manager in his sexy suit." The *Dish* reporter would eat it up, and probably nibble on Harlan too.

He growls, and the hand on my back swoops down over my ass. "Careful."

I grin. There's my slightly uncivilized Dom. "You can spank me later. For now, talk to me."

He cuddles me in, and we sway together in something that isn't so much a dance of bodies, but feels like a dance of hearts. "I have a really good life. A job I love, friends who go to the mat for me, things that stretch me and make me feel good every day."

I smile, because he's so speaking the words of my soul. "Yeah, me too."

He nuzzles his cheek against mine. "And then you showed up and I see holes I didn't know existed." He reaches for my fingers, interlacing them slowly. "Do you have any idea how long it's been since I walked down the street holding some-one's hand?"

He's breaking me wide open with the aching wonder in his words. "We should maybe try doing that in broad daylight."

His entire body stills.

He taught me to ask. To say the words. "Be my guy, Harlan."

Chapter Forty-Eight

HARLAN

Be my guy.

I freeze. Being her guy is totally different than being her Dom.

She looks up at me and her heart is in her eyes. "Hang out at my apartment with me and eat pizza and binge-watch bad TV. Help me find a couch we won't break. Walk on the beach with me so we can freeze our asses off and then find a fun way to warm up. Be my guy, Harlan—not just my Dom."

I can't breathe. She's totally assaulted all the walls I have left. I kneel down on the floor, since that's where I feel like I'm headed anyhow, and pull her into my arms.

This is not a scene. This is a man and a woman and there are no rules and no safewords and nothing in my training remotely knows what to do. But I do. I hold her to my heart, because that's the only part of me left that knows how to speak and let the impossible tenderness that lives there wrap around both of us.

And then I pick her up and sling her over my shoulder, because we are so done here.

I don't stop at the laughter behind me, or the helpfully

shouted suggestions that will probably shock all the poor vanilla folks who were brave enough to come here tonight. I don't even stop as Scorpio's ass wiggles on my shoulder. I need her, and I need her right now, and I'm done with everything and everyone standing in the way of that.

She asked me what I want, and I don't know all the answers yet—but I know some. It's time to let her see them.

The bellhop's eyes bug out of his head when I round the corner with Scorpio over my shoulder, but he scurries to push the elevator button for me. The doors slide open just as we arrive. I wait for them to close before I slide my gorgeous, disheveled woman into my arms.

Her eyes are huge, and I can see her biting back questions.

I lean down to kiss her. "This isn't a scene, beautiful, at least not yet. Ask whatever you want."

"Where are we going?"

I laugh, because the bubbling happiness inside me needs somewhere to go. "Up."

She punches my bicep, hard enough to impress me with her right hook. "And after that?"

To everywhere possible. "You'll see." The elevator pings and opens on a small foyer. Four doors. The penthouse suites. I pick the one furthest left and swipe my thumb across the biometric scan.

The door opens slowly, and I watch Scorpio's face as she catches her first glimpse of what lies inside. A slow, astonished inhale, and then her eyes are on mine, full of questions.

I touch the silky smoothness of the small of her back and nudge her forward.

She steps in with the slow dignity of a princess or a wedding processional. And then she stops.

I know what she sees. The music, the candlelight, the rose

petals. Simple and not very imaginative—but all of it done by my hands.

She's looking around. Taking it all in. "You had this all set up. Before."

She doesn't have to say before what. I'll never forget her words. *Be my guy.* "Yeah."

She's grinning. "You know, we've never actually had sex."

I groan, and it's all I can do to keep my hands off her. "You think I don't know that?"

She spins to face me and her eyes are lit up with soft, embarrassed joy. "You did this for me. For our first time together."

"You deserve soft and sexy and romantic." And she wants it, which matters a hell of a lot more. "I know I don't usually come across as the guy who wants that, or who can provide it."

She snorts. "You mean the guy with the big marshmallow heart under his tats? Do you think I'm blind?"

I growl, which just makes her laugh. She leans up and kisses me. "Tough guy."

It's time to show her the best part. "Take one more look, because it's going to be a while before we're back down here."

I feel her surprise, but I don't answer it. I take her hand instead. I'm done with words. For the rest of tonight, it's all about showing her.

Chapter Forty-Nine

SCORPIO

I have no idea where we're going, but he does. Up the winding staircase in the corner of our suite to a small landing space and a door. He pushes it open and the cold of a fall Seattle night rushes in.

His lips touch my shoulder. "Trust me."

I absolutely do.

He takes me out onto the rooftop, and I'm expecting cold, but it isn't at all. The heat registers first, the warmth emanating from magical outdoor columns of fire and light. And in the midst of them—a bed. An enormous one piled high with quilts and pillows and decadence.

The kind of bed where promises are made.

And promises are kept.

A cold breeze sneaks in to brush against my nipples, the slinky gold dress no barrier at all, and Harlan's hands aren't far behind. "Cold?"

His body is pressing into me from behind, and sometime in the last minute he's lost his jacket and his shirt. I lean back into his warmth. "No."

His fingers are doing devilish things to my nipples. "I want to take you over to that big bed and make love to you until neither of us can move anymore. But first I'm going to bend you over against that railing and take you fast and hard where everyone can hear. I need to be inside you."

I have no idea if we're in a scene or not and I don't care. I push my ass back against his erection, begging. "Please."

He's already moving, taking us both to where he wants us, putting my hands down on the cold metal rail of the rooftop that overlooks all of Seattle. "Hold on here." He runs his hands down my arms, down my back, sliding my dress up over my head and my panties down my legs. I feel the cool wind blow over my exposed parts and then his fingers dive into my dripping pussy. The sound he makes is profane, and totally sacred.

He bends down behind me, licking me as he slides my feet out of my shoes and up onto some kind of blocks. Stepping stones. Raising me up to exactly the height he needs.

The man came seriously prepared.

I can hear myself keening, whimpering, letting him know with every sound how badly I need him inside me. Letting all of Seattle hear. This magic can't be anything but goodness in the world.

He gives my pussy a light swat, and then he's licking me from behind again, drinking me up, and it's all I can do to stay on my feet. His hands move up my thighs, holding me, spreading me further open to his tongue. "You taste like heaven, beautiful."

I have no words left. I just moan and lean back into his face. Slow can come later.

His hands have no mercy. They demand that I stay right where he's put me and let his tongue ravage me and careen myself into the screaming orgasm he's driving my way.

If anyone in Seattle is listening, I hope they have a sexy friend nearby.

I nearly bang my head on the railing I come so hard, and then he's up behind me, and I'm reaching back for the beautiful slide of his cock into me, crying out from the epic rightness of it. He pulls my chest up, kissing my neck and ravishing my breasts and holding my hips as he rocks inside me.

I take one timeless moment to breathe in what it is to be filled by this man—and then I lean forward, grab the rails with everything I've got, and tilt my hips in desperate demand.

His hands land on me, and then all that exists is the wet, slapping music of his body driving into mine, his hips melding with my ass, his cock moving fast and fierce and deep inside me.

I hear the savage noises that must be his, and then realize they're mine. His hands grip my hips even harder, and the sounds that rise out of his throat to meet mine are all I need. I let go, launching the million pieces of me into the sky and pleading with him to come with me.

Together we rise, we rage, we explode into each other.

I don't let go of the railing, knowing that it and his still-pulsing cock are all that are keeping me on my feet. And then even that isn't enough, and I'm liquid, human goo who's only standing because he's being all my bones. His arm cradles me into his chest, holding tighter. I arch my hips, rocking backward, because he's still hard inside me and I'm not nearly done with feeling that.

"Shh." His other hand plays in the dripping folds around my clit as he rocks with me, tiny thrusts that feel like they reach all the way to my heart. "Easy. Just hold still and let me send you over again while I'm inside you like this."

I want to protest, to tell him I can't stand any more, that there's no blood left to feed my brain. Instead, I can feel my body responding to his fingers. Readying for him—a slow, quivering tide of molten fire this time.

"That's it, beautiful. Let me hear you."

Even my whimpers are soft now. Begging sighs and breathy whispers and need so huge and so tender and so open that all I can do is drape myself over this man and give everything I am to his fingers.

His breathing in my ear is choppy, desperate, reverent.

When I come, rippling around his hardness, it feels like a prayer.

I don't know how I get both of us to the bed, but somehow I do.

I don't bother with covers. The hotel manager wasn't wrong—his heaters are magic. There's just enough sharpness in the air to keep us from combusting.

I lay Scorpio down long enough to switch out one condom for another one, and then I give her pussy a lick and a promise and slide my way back up her silky body. "I swear I'll find some finesse later. Right now I just need to be back inside you."

She's already tipping her hips to meet me and this time I can see her eyes as I enter her. Liquid pools of desire and welcome and everything I had no idea I wanted.

I slide in, balls deep, and then I stop, because I want to be in exactly this moment and cherish it. Cherish her.

She breathes into it with me and her eyes never leave mine. They just glisten.

She's everything—and she's mine.

I start to move, the cool air of the night on my back and the spiraling heat of what we're making between us everywhere else. I pull her knees up, shifting the angles so I can slide in deeper. Her eyes haze as I hit exactly the right spot inside her.

I take it slow until she whimpers in protest, and then I do what I've wanted to do since the first time she brought me cookies. I thrust deep into her, over and over and over again, and watch her eyes as she shatters.

Mine. It's the last thought I have before I go with her.

I don't know how long it takes to breathe again, or to work out where my sweaty, satisfied body ends and hers begins. I shift a little, testing to see what body parts still work, and chuckle as she lets out a squawk of protest and locks her ankles behind my back.

Feisty sub.

I pull out, leaving my fingers in her pussy just long enough to do the condom-switching thing again, and shake my head. At this rate, I'm going to have to sneak out for a middle-of-the-night resupply—and I packed like an optimistic teenager.

I slide back in before my cock can get too sad about his missing playmate. I watch her face, looking for any signs she's getting tender. She squeezes her inner muscles around me, her nipples hardening under her cami in the cool night air.

I want those too, and tonight I don't plan to deny myself anything at all. I hold on and roll us over, keeping my hands on her hips just long enough for her to figure out gravity has moved, and then I have the cami off and her breasts in my hands.

She grinds on top of me, gorgeous and needy and clearly still seeking the same thing I am.

More.

She slides her hands up my chest and then pauses, looking down and grinning. "How did I not know you have a nipple ring?"

I pull her down and kiss her nose. "Because it's mostly been you getting naked."

She raises an eyebrow. "I've seen your naked chest and it totally wasn't there."

"I haven't worn it for a while. Got all dolled up for you tonight."

She's laughing, but she's also squiggling down to lap it with her tongue.

My cock isn't happy about his lost playmate, so I take advantage of the distraction to slide a finger in her ass.

She squeaks and tries to bat me away.

I growl. "You're mine, beautiful. Anywhere, anyhow, anytime." We might be having some pretty damn vanilla sex and I might be ridiculously enjoying myself, but my Dom wants in on this too and her ass is right at the top of his list of pleasures. I tug a pillow under my head, because this I'm definitely going to want to watch. "Turn around and straddle me with your ass this way so that I can put my fingers and my cock into you at the same time."

She points a pouty look at my nipple ring, but she's already shifting her legs around. I keep sliding my finger in and out of her ass, and I love how she's fumbling as she turns.

Hell, there's nothing about this I don't love.

Chapter Fifty-One

SCORPIO

I slide down on Harlan's cock and waiting fingers, and shake my head as he takes me into yet another new land. One where I feel full and exposed and watched and entirely wanton.

I hope the whole city is catching a ride on whatever this is, because it feels that big.

I rock my ass back on his fingers, needing more. He growls and slaps his other hand down on my hip. "Slow down, woman, because this is the sexiest thing I've ever seen and I want it to last more than three seconds."

I have way more faith in his self-control than that, but I tilt my ass back like he's guiding me to do, and hold as still as I can while he slides two fingers in and out of my ass. It lights up nerves I don't even know I have, and makes it so I can feel every inch of his cock, even though I'm barely moving.

His free hand moves to rub circles on my ass cheek, his thumb pressing close to where his other fingers are moving in and out. "Tell me what you want, beautiful."

I want too many things. I want to see his face and I want it to last forever and I want the orgasm that is coming for me as badly as I want my next breath. "Tell me what you see."

I can hear his quick intake of air. I've surprised him.

I've surprised me, but I want to be every kind of intimate with this man, and that includes knowing more of what lives inside his head.

His fingers keep up their deadly work riling up my ass. "I see your wet pussy wrapped around my cock, and it's reminding me how good you taste and how long I waited to be with you this way. You're redder than you were half an hour ago, and swollen, and it makes me feel like a caveman in the best way to know I did that to you. Your ass cheeks are rocking as my fingers slide inside you, and knowing that you're letting me watch you like this is pretty much the hottest thing ever." He stops, chuckling as I gush wetter on his cock. "I was lying here feeling all embarrassed about my clunky words and then you go and do that and I feel pretty much like a god."

I want, so badly, to see his face, but the picture he's painting is so freaking erotic and gorgeous that I can't move.

"I'm going to make you come now, beautiful. I want to feel you fucking explode all over me."

I have just long enough for my insides to gush again and then he's thrusting his cock up into me in time with his fingers and I can't form coherent thoughts anymore. I can only fly, shooting up on the track he's laying for me.

I tilt back my head and howl at the sky. And then I detonate.

When I come back to planet Earth, I'm tucked under warm covers with Harlan's arm under my head and his thighs under one of mine and a very happy throbbing between my legs.

He trails his fingers lightly over me, leaving light trails of flame everywhere.

I curl closer, inarticulately happy.

He holds some small nibble up to my mouth and I open

obediently. It tastes like breakfast in a tiny little bite—eggs and bacon and everything good. I shimmy over to the tray with the food and pick up one that looks the same and feed it to him, grinning. "This is not the kind of food you feed your lover when you plan to roll over and go to sleep."

He kisses my cheek and feeds me another nibble. "Nope. Keep your strength up."

It's not strength fueling this night. This time I roll over to get at the food and his hand slides between my thighs like it lives there. "Sore?"

Yes. No. I roll back and pop more food in his mouth. "I'll tell you if I need us to shift gears any."

He's still stroking, and it makes me feel like a happily demented kitten. "I'm going to carry you downstairs soon."

I can see that the magic heaters are starting to gutter. "Thank you. This was amazing."

He kisses me, and there's more demand this time. "This is just getting started, beautiful. Eat up—you're going to need it."

Chapter Fifty-Two

HARLAN

It's warmer inside, and it smells like rose petals.

I make it to the bottom of the winding staircase without landing either of us on our asses, and breathe a sigh of relief. I plan to spend the rest of this night happily horizontal.

I toss the woman in my arms onto the bed just to hear her squeak at me again. She sprawls exactly where she's landed, wide open to me and eyes full of laughing desire.

I dive for her, landing tickling fingers on her ribs as I dip my head between her legs.

She screams, and her legs slam together around my ears.

I grin and flick her clit with my tongue. "It's going to take way more than that to keep me out of your pussy. Open up."

She glares down at me. "I want more kisses first. And no tickling."

Bossy sub. I slide up her body, tasting as I go. She sucks in a choked breath as I close my teeth over one of her nipples, and I decide she can have her kisses in a bit. I torment her nipples until she's practically hissing, and then I lick my way up her collarbone to the soft skin of her neck and the hopelessly ticklish region just below her ear.

When she's a mess of helpless, laughing desire, I slide into her pussy again. And then I just lie still, because something about her warmth wrapped around me is so good that it's all I need.

She rocks ever so gently, stretching her legs out along mine. I pick up the rhythm of her rocking, some kind of primal, soft dance that has nothing to do with sex and everything to do with joining to her and all of who she is. She kisses me, feather light touches on my face, my neck, my shoulders, as her fingers trail down my back, drawing lazy circles on my ass cheeks.

We could do this forever and never come and it would be perfect.

I breathe into this new experience and this new life I've suddenly found and I hear her breath moving with mine. Our ribs, floating on the same lazy ocean of sensory pleasure and something far deeper. I feel the smile rising all the way up from my toes.

Being her guy is going to be the best thing I've ever done.

Chapter Fifty-Three

SCORPIO

I feel his heartbeat, the slow, steady pulse of it. The lake of calm, satisfied, beautiful man draped over me.

And then I feel him quicken.

I grin at him and at the sudden playful lust in his eyes. "Are we going to sleep at all tonight?"

He's doing something wicked to my nipples with his fingers. "For the foreseeable future, plan to nap on the couch or under your desk at work. If you're in the same bed I am, you're not going to be sleeping much."

That sounds impossible. And holy. "We'll break something."

He rolls to the side and cups me, gently rocking his fingers. "My fingers will never get tired of playing with your pussy."

I am absolutely certain there are no more orgasms in me. There isn't even a decent squirm. "I'm done, sexy man. You've wrung me totally dry."

His chuckle beside me is low and amused. "Bets?"

The rocking is already stirring things up, but I have a rep to maintain. "Totally. What do I get if I win?"

"Hmmm. There's a really big spa bathtub around the

corner. I think I'll lay you down over the edge on some soft towels with your legs in a tub full of hot bubbles. And then I'll climb in and lick you until the water goes cold."

I groan. I've already made plans to have a hot, steamy affair with his tongue. "That's some really excellent motivation. What do you get if you win?" Because he's already making it really obvious he's going to.

He nips my earlobe. "The bathtub thing, except I get to fuck you after I lick you."

I spread my legs and let my hips move against the slow, insistent, stupidly effective rocking of his hand. "I hope your plans for tomorrow don't involve me being able to walk."

He grins. "Nope. Or the next day either." He slides two fingers inside me and strokes the spot that has apparently risen from the dead. Chasing what he wants with infinite patience— and infinite demand.

But it's not his fingers that have me now. It's his eyes, looking deep into me and offering everything he has. He stays that way as his fingers carry me right to where he wants me to be. And then he leans down and kisses my cheek, feather light. "Come for me now, love."

I smile as I go over the edge he's brought me to, the glistening, glorious one that will never make me bleed. The one where he'll be waiting on the other side.

The one where he will be my guy—and I will be his love.

Chapter Fifty-Four

EPILOGUE - HARLAN

I put down what's left of my slice of pizza. One hunger taken care of.

The other one is apparently bottomless.

I run my slightly greasy, very appreciative fingers over the lusciously naked woman who's cuddled up next to me on the couch, watching the movie we've been trying to watch for three days. I wait until the scene mostly finishes and then I nuzzle into her neck. It's become one of my favorite addictions. "So there's this guy I know at the club."

She laughs and pauses the movie. "Threesomes are a hard limit."

I growl. "They better be." I've never shared well, but this woman takes that to a whole new level. "He's a drummer. And Quint plays some guitar. They've been talking."

She's eyeing me now, in that suspicious way I hope she never loses, because someone needs to keep me on my toes— and because I never want to stop surprising her.

I grin and fondle her naked ass. "Ari wants to do some nights at the club with live music. Which means we need a band who won't freak out if there are screams from the dungeon."

She's catching up now. "You want me to join a BDSM band?"

I shrug, surprised I'm having trouble reading her. "I'm busy working the floor most nights, so I thought it might give you something to do."

She sits up and straddles me, and I can tell by the fiercely amused look on her face that she's not swallowing any of my crap. "This is you thinking you know what I need in my life and trying to sneak it by me when I'm weak from pizza and too much sex."

Pretty much. "Guilty. Sorry." She's made very clear that she wants the man as much as she wants the Dom, and there are lines. Which I keep crossing. "It would be a low-key gig, a chance to have some music in your life with a couple of guys I won't need to kill, and I'd get to hear you sing." Which is another addiction I'm rapidly growing, even if right now it's mostly only in the shower.

She's rubbing herself slowly up and down my cock, which seems to be having second thoughts on his planned nap. "There would need to be some rules."

I growl and hold her hips still. "We need to have another chat about topping from the bottom, beautiful."

She laughs. "I'm on top right now. And you're avoiding my rules."

She's warm and wet and if I lift her a few inches we can have this discussion while she's riding my cock. I do the deed and groan as I slide in. We've done the tests and ditched the condoms, and this right here is pretty much my definition of heaven.

She slaps my hands off her hips and holds herself as primly as she can with a cock balls deep in her pussy. "Rules. No scening while I'm singing. That means no plugs, no clamps, no skimpy outfits."

She's still too new to understand all the doors she's left open. I man up and close them for her. "Okay. I'll keep my distractions minimal."

She grinds a tight, sexy circle and snickers. "You have no idea what that word means, tough guy."

I grin and thrust up into her a few times. "Sure I do. It means you don't want to squeak while you sing."

She splutters and gives my nipple ring a tug. "I don't squeak."

I want to fuck her until she's very convinced of the error of that statement, but teasing Scorpio is one of my very favorite things, and this orgasm isn't coming nearly as soon as she thinks it is. "Any ideas yet about where we should go on our vacation?" We've booked the same week off and I don't intend to spend it on her couch, no matter how much I like it here.

She leans down and her eyes have that soft, melty look in them that still slays me, every damn time. "Somewhere we can hold hands in daylight."

I catch her fingers in mine, because that's become one of my favorite things and she knows it. And thrust up into her, just so she doesn't forget my other favorite thing. "That's not going to get us plane tickets."

She grins. "You're so bossy."

Not anymore. Someone has lulled her man into lazy, lustful complacency.

The love part—that's all on me.

Chapter Fifty-Five
EPILOGUE - SCORPIO

This whole talking-while-fucking thing is just plain weird, and we do it all the damn time. He slides into me at the breakfast table, in the shower, while we're watching bad TV, while I'm reading. Not to interrupt whatever I'm doing. Not to have sex. Just to be inside me.

Eating Cheerios with a hard cock in my pussy is definitely a new relationship experience.

He says it's all about being totally present in the in-betweens.

I stroke his cheek, because much as I want him to bend me over the couch right now and fuck me silly, there's something I want more. This deep, everyday closeness that I'm learning to crave more than chocolate and sex and music combined.

But I have a rep to maintain. I tighten my inner muscles around him in the way I know he likes.

He growls.

The man is getting very good at making me beg. Or, in this case, answer his question, because that's almost always the surest path to getting what I want. "I was thinking a beach. Ideally one where naked and alone happens a lot."

"Mmmm. I like the sounds of that." He slides backward on the couch far enough to prop himself partway up to sitting. All the better to fondle me. And to put our eyes on the same level. The man is the master of subtle power cues. Growling or not, right now he's not my Dom—he's just a guy with a naked woman in his lap who wants to go on a sandy vacation. "Maybe somewhere we can still get restaurant food."

I snort. "What, you're sick of eggs already?" It's about the only thing either of us can cook.

He grins at me. "Gabby's going to give cooking lessons. I set it up with Damon."

I laugh so damn often with this man's cock inside me. "In Fettered's kitchen?"

He nods solemnly. "We Doms need to keep our skills up."

At any other club that class would be put on for the subs. "You're a smart and very sexy man, tough guy."

He kisses me, long and intently, and I can feel his cock pulsing inside me. Now we're getting somewhere.

I nuzzle into his cheek and lay out my best bait. "Ari's coming over soon. We should probably put some clothes on."

He growls. "Define 'soon.'"

I have no idea, but she's smart enough to knock. And to go get coffee if she can hear his hand meeting my ass. "Probably not enough time. I know we've tired you out."

He snorts. "Somebody wants a spanking."

I bend down and mouth his nipple ring. "I totally do. How much harder do I have to work at it?"

He grins at me and thrusts a little harder. "I think I'll just wait until Ari leaves so I can add on everything you earn while she's here." He reaches around behind me and slides a finger in my ass. "And because she's your friend, you get a swat for every time she's sassy too."

I can't help it—I start laughing, even though I'm close

enough to coming that I'm going to be squeaking soon. "That is so not fair." And absolutely my Dom giving me what I want.

He squeezes my nipple in time with the finger sliding in and out of my ass. "You can always tell her it's your ass on the line and she should be on her best behavior."

I bite his earlobe. "Right. Because that will totally make her behave."

His fingers move faster. I arch my back, trying to put more of me into both of his hands.

He stops dead, pops me off his cock and onto his lap, and kisses my nose. "Go put on clothes. Ari will be here soon."

My entire body wails at him. "I need to come, dammit."

He raises an eyebrow, all arrogant Dom. "Be good or I won't let you come tonight either."

I want to sulk like a two year old, but I'm not sure I can handle the consequences. "That's just plain mean."

He leans over and whispers in my ear, "When she leaves, I want you in the shower, naked and waiting for me."

My shower with the new, very sexy renovations. I climb off his lap and reach for the lacy underwear that seems to breed overnight when I'm not looking. I pull it on slowly and then reach for his t-shirt. I have a thing lately for being able to smell him when he's not around.

He grins and stands up. "I'm going to go take a nap. Naked."

I shake my head. "You are an evil, evil man." One who obviously isn't going to let me sleep again tonight.

A man keeping his promises. Every last one of them.

Chapter Fifty-Six
HARLAN

I probably have no business being here. Scorpio's a big girl, and at least one of the Doms in her new band is green enough that he still thinks I'm scary.

Quint strolls into the lounge and raises an eyebrow at me. "You can't sing worth shit. Beat it."

I flick my eyes over to where Scorpio's sitting on a stool, jawing with Jackson and his drums. "I'm just here to keep an eye on my woman."

He snorts. "You're here to make sure three Doms can handle her."

He's not entirely wrong about that. "She's used to running the show on the music stuff."

Quint leans against the wall next to me. "And here I was planning to go all Dom on her ass."

I growl, but I don't mean it. The day might come where I stop overreacting about all things Scorpio, but it hasn't arrived yet. "Sorry."

He grins. "Ari already threatened me with zombie paperwork if I fuck with her."

That's probably way more effective than me skulking on a

wall and looking like I might wave my fists around. I'm useless here and I know it, but I want the woman sitting on a stool razzing her new drummer to have everything. And I just can't see my way to that happening without music.

Even in the shower, she sings like her life depends on it.

Which means she needs a band, and at least this one is full of guys I don't have to kill.

The front door pushes open and Eli walks into the lounge, a keyboard over one shoulder and a pile of wires and metal parts over the other. Ari's hot on his heels, carrying the most oversized violin case of all time. I'm smart enough to let her keep lugging it—my ears are still ringing from the last time I tried to take something out of her hands when she didn't want me to.

Quint pushes off the wall. "That's my cue."

Ari sets down what must be a cello and then joins me against the wall. There's a flurry of activity as mikes and amps and who knows what else are plugged in and tested, and then suddenly the logistics are done and it's just four people sizing each other up and wondering what they've just landed in.

I read the body language like the pro I am and hide my grin. They might be three Doms and a sub in the bedroom, but Jackson and Eli have clearly already decided where they plan to be in this particular hierarchy. They've both taken seats behind their respective instruments and are watching Scorpio and Quint with interest.

Waiting to see who's in charge.

Quint slides his guitar strap over his head and nods at the mike in the center. "You're up, lady. Pick a song and take us through it."

Scorpio's eyebrows nearly bounce off her hairline. "That's the lead singer's job."

"Yup." He strums a couple of quiet chords. "Eli's decent at harmonies. Jackson and I can't sing worth shit."

My sub looks ready to pound him into sand. "I'm a backup singer."

"Not anymore, you're not."

Ari snickers. Quint's not using his Dom voice, but it's close enough that we both know there's no point arguing.

Scorpio's not so smart. "I'll do lead guitar, but someone else has to run this thing."

Quint just keeps quietly strumming.

I keep watching my woman, not at all sure whether she's going to go for it. There's a big difference between being the heart of the band and being someone who steps in and plays guitar a few nights a week.

Ari's eyes are glued to the action. "Did you put him up to this?"

I keep my voice very quiet. "No."

"She's going to pitch a fit when she figures out how well he sings."

I'm still watching my sub. Her eyes are studying Quint like he arrived special delivery from the nice aliens in the hovering spaceship.

Ari squints at the band, trying to spy whatever it is that I see.

I smile when it lands. "She's just figured out why Quint wants it this way." A man who wants this to be the one small part of his life where he's not the guy holding the reins.

Ari laughs, because she's obviously figured it out too. She pushes off the wall. "Hey, Scorpio! I know what you should call your band."

My sub looks over, scowl all over her face. "It's not my band."

Quint is smart enough to be eyeing Ari with extreme suspicion. "We'll name it."

Ari flashes him a grin. "You'll pick something descriptive and stupid like Four People with Instruments."

That's a low blow. And a correct one.

Ari heads for the door with the kind of shit-eating grin that says she has this utterly, totally in the bag. When she's two steps away, she tosses words back over her shoulder. "I'll go put you guys on the schedule for next Friday night." She pauses, with a switch's sense of impeccable timing. "Opening night for Doms on the Bottom."

Chapter Fifty-Seven

SCORPIO

Dammit, this isn't supposed to be funny.

I glare at Jackson, who's manfully trying to get his snorts under control. Eli and Quint aren't even bothering. Which is freaking kryptonite to my ability to say no, because they clearly all have a sense of humor and there's pretty much nothing that's more important to good band dynamics, at least any band I'm a part of.

There's just one problem. I don't know if I can do this.

Playing music was so big for me. An ocean of big, one I knew how to go deep in, nearly drown in, lost friends in. I've tinkered a bit with a guitar in my hands since, done some jamming, but it's not the same. Too much like trying to have sex with clothes on.

I only know how to do music naked.

Especially if I'm the one running the show, and right now I'm looking at three guys who think that's an awesome idea. Who all appear totally happy to lie back and have someone else in charge.

I slide my fingers up and down Lightning's frets. The energy's building inside me, the need to let the music go full blast and with all of who I am, because that's really the only way I know how to play it. I run through the very short list of songs I'm willing to try to sing lead on with no prep. It's tempting to fire straight into some Led Zeppelin or Jimi Hendrix and dare them all to keep up, but that would be me heading for a sharp edge just because I can.

Thanks to the man skulking on the back wall, I don't need to do that anymore.

So instead, I play the opening chords of a classic Elton John ballad. The kind of deceptively simple song that will let me figure out pretty quickly just what the guys behind me can do.

Because I can feel this thing. It's turning into mine and I haven't even opened my mouth yet.

Jackson grabs the beat first, which I expected, but he keeps it simple and quiet, which I didn't. Eli surprises me by diving for his cello, but I know better than to argue with a man about what instrument he wants to play. Quint grins and layers in a chord progression under mine that makes us sound damn good for two people who haven't even gotten to first base yet.

Damn.

I run us through the opening bars a couple more times, letting everyone settle in, and then I clear my throat, lean into the mike, and sing the opening lines. Eli's right with me on the harmonies, and so is Quint. With a nice, gravelly baritone that could do lead singer in a heartbeat.

Rat bastard.

But this scene is already rolling, and I know I have two choices. Play, or safeword out. And Lightning is damn sick of being my brakes. I turn forward, face the room that won't be empty as soon as we have a half-dozen recognizable songs we can play. Sex might be something I mostly do in private, but this never has been.

Harlan's watching us from the wall, and it's not the lust that surprises me, or even his tapping foot. It's the simple, shining happiness in his eyes.

The guy gets off on making me happy.

Jackson drives us into the chorus with a tricky, understated beat that says I don't know half of what he can do yet, and Quint waits for my cue on the guitar. I keep to simple chords. Eli's cello is doing something beautiful and a little primal underneath us all, and it will fit the vibe of Fettered down to the ground.

I close my eyes and let the music swallow me.

If a simple ballad can do this to me, the first time we do pounding rock is going to break me wide open.

Which is going to be totally okay. I shouldn't have worried. I have four Doms—three playing, and one watching from the shadows—all totally willing to hold the walls up so that I can let go.

And nobody will bleed unless they want to.

I hit a chord progression that has Quint snorting, and charge into a repeat of the chorus.

We're going to totally rock this thing.

———

Get DESIRE, where cookie-baking grandma meets Dom—and the heat is definitely not in the kitchen.

(If you can't follow a link from here, go to liliamoon.com and I'll get you hooked up.)

xoxo Lilia

Printed in Great Britain
by Amazon